MERRY CHRISTMAS, BABY

Katie Reus

Cover art: Jaycee of Sweet 'N Spicy Designs
JRT Editing
Author website: http://www.katiereus.com

Merry Christmas, Baby/Katie Reus. -- 1st ed.
KR Press, LLC

ISBN-10: 1-942447-85-X
ISBN-13: 978-1-942447-85-6

For those who believe in the magic of the holidays.

Praise for the novels of Katie Reus

Continued...

"A sexy, well-crafted paranormal romance that succeeds with smart characters and creative world building."—Kirkus Reviews

"*Mating Instinct*'s romance is taut and passionate . . . Katie Reus's newest installment in her Moon Shifter series will leave readers breathless!"
—Stephanie Tyler, *New York Times* bestselling author

"Both romantic and suspenseful, a fast-paced sexy book full of high stakes action." —Heroes and Heartbreakers

"Katie Reus pulls the reader into a story line of second chances, betrayal, and the truth about forgotten lives and hidden pasts."
—The Reading Café

"Nonstop action, a solid plot, good pacing, and riveting suspense."
—RT Book Reviews

"Sexy suspense at its finest."
—Laura Wright, *New York Times* bestselling author of *Branded*

The bell above the front door to Nora's Books and Brew jingled, but Nora didn't bother to glance away from the customer she was helping. Since renovating this place seven months ago it was no longer just a bookstore, but a combination bookstore and coffee shop and they sold more coffee than books. Which wasn't exactly surprising since Holly, North Carolina saw a lot of tourists, especially during December. Located in the Blue Ridge Mountains, it was a popular tourist getaway that boasted cobblestone streets, Victorian gingerbread architecture and an old-world feel that made her never want to leave. And it was Christmas twenty-four-seven, year round. Nora's friend Ella, the town scrooge, hated it, but after growing up with a mom who got depressed every damn holiday and refused to do anything special for either of her daughters, Nora loved everything about Holly.

"Trust me, your daughter, no matter what age, will love the elf, even if she doesn't read the book. My sister's seventeen and goes crazy with this thing. Every morning I find him in a different place around the house."

The woman with pale blonde hair and a bright smile nodded. "I'll take two sets and a pound of the White Christmas coffee. Whole beans."

"I'll meet you at the cash register." Even though the town was Christmas-themed year round, the month of December was still always their busiest. In addition to her regular employees, she'd hired three seasonal ones, all high-school students, to help out in the afternoons. They were all busy so she headed to the back to grab the Elf on the Shelf book sets and the coffee.

As she passed Macy and Eleanor Baker, sisters in their sixties barely a year apart, sitting at one of the high-top tables in the café, she paused at the odd way they were watching her. "What? Do I have something on my face?" She'd been working since eight o'clock this morning and had barely taken a bathroom break.

Macy, the brunette, gave her a Cheshire cat smile. "Nope. Though it wouldn't hurt you to put some lipstick on."

Nora blinked in surprise.

Eleanor nudged her sister. "Don't be rude. She looks fine. He won't care about lipstick anyway."

He? Since she had no idea what they were talking about, Nora gave them a polite smile, murmured something about grabbing stock from the back, and kept going. She adored the sisters, but they could be eccentric on their best days. And today, she didn't have time for their dose of crazy. She slipped behind the counter, the rich aroma of coffee, coconut, vanilla, caramel and nuts all filling the air. The scents were soothing and familiar, as were the little beeps from the cash register as Kelsey rang up another customer. Music to Nora's ears.

MERRY CHRISTMAS, BABY | 9

"I'll grab what you need. I overheard you and the snow bunny. Two elf sets and coffee, right?" Marjorie, one of her full-time employees asked as she pushed open the swinging door to the back.

"Yeah, but you don't have to—"

"Go see your man. I got this." Marjorie tilted her chin in the direction of the café before disappearing through the door.

What the heck? Nora turned around and froze for just a second. Jackson O'Connor, Mr. Too-sexy-for-his-own-good stood at the high-top table talking to the Baker sisters. He held a bouquet of white snapdragons, her favorite. Her immediate instinct was to duck in the back and just avoid seeing him, but screw him. He was in her territory and she certainly didn't want his flowers. So she pasted on her "shopkeeper smile" and skirted around the counter.

As she rounded it, he looked over, those striking blue eyes landing on her. And damn it, she felt the effect of that stare all the way to her toes. She tried to pretend she didn't, but her body didn't lie. Everything around her funneled out, the rich scents and chattering customers all seemed to fade away as she maneuvered her way through the tables. She wished she was in something sexier than jeans, a red and green striped top and her apron, but there was nothing she could do about it. Now she understood the lipstick comment, but not the 'your man' one. Jackson certainly wasn't hers.

He'd made that perfectly clear with his radio silence over the last three weeks. One date and he'd completely ghosted on her; no calls, nothing. Considering they'd been friends before their date, it cut deep that he'd simply decided to ignore her for no reason she could decipher.

"O'Connor," she said politely as she reached the table. Oh yeah, it was back to O'Connor, what pretty much everyone in town called him. Calling him Jackson was way too intimate and she wanted to set up clear boundaries between them.

She saw the slight way his eyes narrowed when she did. "You have a few seconds, Nora?" His voice was deep and delicious, the baritone making all her nerve endings flare to life.

"Ah..." She glanced behind her. The line at the register wasn't too bad, but the truth was, she didn't want to talk to him, much less see him. "I'm pretty busy."

"Oh go on, honey." Macy winked at her. "No one will blame you for taking a few minutes to yourself."

"And if she's not interested, we are," Eleanor continued.

To Nora's surprise, Jackson's cheeks flushed red. Clearing his throat, he motioned toward the front door. "I shouldn't have come at such a busy time."

Though she wanted to tell him that he was right—and give him a piece of her mind—she simply smiled and headed for the front door with him. "Don't worry about it." She had to keep her "shopkeeper smile" in place until they were alone. Otherwise everyone in town would gossip and though she might hate it, she had to uphold a certain appearance. When she was Nora Cassidy, business owner, she had to keep a smile on her face and be professional at all times. Which normally wasn't hard at all. She loved her job and she loved the people of Holly.

"That's the fakest smile I've ever seen," Jackson murmured as he held the door open for her.

The bell jingled overhead as a blast of wintry air rolled over her. She shivered, wrapped her arms around herself as her boots crunched over the icy sidewalk. And she kept the smile in place even as she gritted out, "No joke. What are you doing here?"

"I..." He practically shoved the flowers at her, the awkward move out of character for the former SEAL. "These are for you."

"They're lovely." Her voice was wry as she reluctantly took them. They really were pretty, but she didn't care. Flowers didn't make up for anything.

"You look a little like you want to throw them in my face." He rubbed a hand over his inky black buzz cut.

She lifted a shoulder. "That would imply I care enough. Look, I've got work to do. We went out and you've made it clear it was a one-time thing. I'm okay with that." Which was a big fat lie. They'd been friends for months, dancing around their attraction until he'd finally asked her out. It wasn't as if they'd been strangers going on a date. No, they'd been way more and he'd just pulled the rug out from under her as if she didn't matter.

"I want to take you out again."

Unable to stop herself, she snorted. "Not interested."

"Nora—"

"No. You can't show up in the middle of one of my busiest days and expect to talk to me about this."

"You're right. I'm sorry. The timing is crappy, I just...I needed to see you. I've missed you."

She blinked, surprised by the sincerity in his voice. But she refused to be swayed by it, not when she was still so hurt.

"Can I call you later?" he continued.

"You can call," she murmured. Didn't mean she'd actually answer. And yeah, she knew she sounded like a complete bitch but she was beyond caring. After one of the hottest nights of her life she'd thought...hell, she hadn't known what she'd thought. That there was a connection between them past just friendship. Something real.

She'd barely dated in the last four years, hadn't been able to. But she'd let Jackson past her defenses, opened up to him, and had almost slept with him. He'd promised to call and for three weeks afterward, *nothing*. She was just glad they hadn't had sex. Well, not technically, because they'd certainly gotten intimate. Holding on to the flowers only because she didn't want any prying eyes to see her give them back to him, she headed back into her shop.

Time to put her game face on and pretend everything was okay, even when it wasn't. A healthy dose of embarrassment and hurt skittered through her and it was all because of him. She was being stupid anyway. It wasn't as if they'd made any commitments to each other or anything. Still, when she'd heard that he'd taken Angelia out days after Nora, it had hit her hard. Not only had Nora and Jackson been friends for months, he'd turned things in another direction and pursued her for weeks as if she was the only thing that mattered to him. Even though she'd been hesitant to cross from friends to more, she'd said yes.

Well she wasn't going to get charmed by him again. No way in hell.

* * *

Jackson scrubbed a hand over his face as he strode down Main Street. He'd screwed up good this time.

Sweet and adorable Nora had barely been able to look at him, much less talk to him. She'd put on a smile, but he knew it hadn't been for him. She just didn't want the locals gossiping. And he couldn't blame her. After their date he'd said things, made promises he meant to keep. Hell, he still planned to keep them. They'd been friends for months and then he'd finally worked up the courage to ask her out. Something he'd never had a problem with before.

Nora was different though; she'd been skittish and he'd wanted everything to go right with her. After their date though, he'd realized that she was it for him—and it had freaked him out. So he'd done the complete cowardly thing and just not called her. Which was, yeah, beyond messed up.

Now that he knew what she looked like when she orgasmed, it was all he'd been able to think about when he'd been talking to her. Or *trying* to talk to her. Around her he got tongue-tied like some teenager. Except he'd never been shy as a teenager. But everything about Nora got him all sorts of twisted up.

Her long, dark wavy hair had been pulled up into a ponytail, but he'd run his fingers through the thick tresses as he claimed her mouth, had sucked on her perfect pink nipples as he stroked her to orgasm with his fingers.

Nope, not continuing that line of thought right now.

Rolling his shoulders once to ease the tension there, he continued down the street, needing to burn off energy before he headed back to his truck a few blocks away.

Garlands and pine wreaths were wrapped around the cast iron street lamps lining Main Street, the scent and sight of Christmas permeated everything in Holly. He'd grown up here, had been dying to move away as soon as he was old enough. Now he couldn't imagine living anywhere else. Especially not since Nora Cassidy had moved to town nine months ago.

She always had a smile on her face for everyone. Until today. She'd covered it up with coldness, but he'd seen the hurt in her gaze and it clawed at him. He would make it up to her, prove that he was sorry. He *had* to.

Flowers had been a lame attempt, but he hadn't been sure how else to break the ice. And what had he been thinking, going to see her when she was busy? He hadn't been thinking, that was the problem. For three weeks he'd managed to avoid her, but today he'd just snapped. The need to see her, to hear her voice, had been overwhelming. As he passed Silver Bells, the combination salon/flower shop—where he'd gotten the snapdragons for Nora, he saw her younger sister Sasha heading his way.

When the seventeen year old spotted him, she immediately broke eye contact and stared straight ahead. Guilt suffused him. He'd gotten to know Sasha over the last few months too. She was Nora's sister and always around. He'd known they were a package deal, especially since Nora had been Sasha's guardian the last four years and he genuinely liked her.

"Sasha," he said quietly, sidestepping a mother pushing a double stroller down the sidewalk.

She gave him the same cold look Nora had, but with the disinterest only a teenager could pull off. "Hey."

"How are you?"

She hiked her backpack against her shoulders, still avoiding his gaze. "Good."

"I fucked up."

Her eyes widened as she met his gaze full-on now. "Dude, you can't say that."

Wincing, he rubbed a hand over his buzz cut. "Sorry, you're right." He was all sorts of twisted up today. What was the matter with him? He'd been a SEAL for a decade and had grown up with two brothers and a sister—who was more a tomboy than anything—so his language was usually rough but she was right. "Maybe don't tell Nora?"

"Whatever. But for the record, you're right. You did screw up. You and her flirted for like, freaking *months*, you pursued her like crazy, then after one date you just fall off the face of the earth. And you've been hooking up with someone else since then? Don't worry, I won't be mentioning your name to my sister. You're not worth her time." She gave a snort of derision before stalking off.

Jackson frowned. He hadn't hooked up with anyone else. Hell, he couldn't think about anyone other than Nora. Hadn't since the day he'd met her. But that wasn't the conversation to have with a seventeen year old kid. Shit, if Sasha thought he was with someone else, then Nora must too.

He had to apologize to her, needed her to listen to him. And he knew if he called her she'd just ignore him. He needed to play this right. He'd already screwed up, maybe too much for her to forgive him.

No, he refused to believe that. He'd been a SEAL. He'd never failed a mission yet and he wasn't going to start now.

CHAPTER TWO

Nora inhaled the fresh scent of hazelnut coffee as she started the economy size coffeemaker. This was her favorite part of the morning; before everyone else showed up it was just her and her shop. The fact that she owned something like this was still hard to wrap her head around.

As she pulled her 'World's Best Sister' mug out of one of the lower cabinets, she realized there were two dirty mugs in one of the industrial sinks. She was the one who'd locked up last night and everything had been clean. A low grade tingling started at the base of her skull. It was probably nothing, but...no, this couldn't be nothing. She was a complete neat freak; she hadn't left this.

Frowning, she did a walk through the coffee shop then moved onto the other half of her place. The bookshelves were divided into genre with romance dominating the majority of her books. It would be impossible to tell if a couple books had been taken on sight, but after she did a walk through all her stock looked fine as did the books. There was a little nook with big throw pillows that looked as if it had been disturbed. She usually tucked the pillows up against the corner wall when she was straightening things at the end of the evening but they'd been pulled out and left on the floor.

Had someone been in here? Only Sasha and a few other employees had keys. She couldn't imagine any of them coming in here without asking. Before she could ponder it a knock at the front door made her nearly jump out of her skin.

When she looked up she saw Jackson standing at the entrance to the bookshop door. Just like that her heart rate kicked up about a thousand notches. She should not be happy to see him, but yeah, her body didn't listen to reason. It was screaming that he must be sincere if he was here again, that she should give him another chance.

Stupid hormones.

A skull cap covered his dark buzz cut. The sharp lines of his face seemed more prominent this morning. He gave her a half-smile that melted her insides as he lifted a small tin of something in one hand. Well, she certainly couldn't leave him standing out in the cold. It had snowed earlier this morning so there was a light dusting over everything.

Hurrying to the door, she opened it and was nearly knocked over by a harsh gust of wind. Her little bell jingled wildly as Jackson stepped inside. "Thanks for letting me in."

"Is everything okay?" she asked, shutting the door behind him. She hated how much his nearness affected her. All her senses just seemed to go into overdrive. She wanted to reach out and cup his cheek, to stroke his soft skin, and feel the way his jaw clenched when she did. But they weren't together, they weren't anything.

"Yeah, I, uh, have a peace offering. And I was hoping you'd have a few minutes to talk before your rush." He held up a small tin with snowmen decorating it.

Her eyes narrowed ever so slightly. "Is that snicker-doodles?"

"Maybe."

Despite her simmering anger at him, she felt herself softening. It was those clear blue eyes that weakened her resolve. The same intense gaze that had sucked her in to begin with. Who was she kidding? It was everything about him. He had a deadly edge to him that made him ridiculously sexy, but he was so sweet. Or he had been the last six months. He'd been coming into her shop pretty much every day until their date. At least the days she'd been working. And he'd made a few custom pieces of furniture for her shop, something that had deeply touched her. She'd paid him, but she knew enough that he'd given her a hefty discount.

Jackson had made her feel special, different. So his to-tal silence after she'd gotten mostly naked with him had yanked that proverbial rug out from under her and she hadn't found her balance since.

"You fight dirty," she murmured, taking the tin from him.

"I play to win." There was something in his tone that made heat flood between her thighs.

She ignored the reaction. "Did Fallon make these?"

"Yep. She said to say hey too."

Nora adored his sister Fallon but for the last few weeks she'd been avoiding Fallon. Which was a totally crappy thing to do but Nora had felt too weird and hadn't wanted to talk about Jackson. And she'd known the subject would come up. "Come on. I've got coffee brewing next door. Let's grab some and you can tell me why you're here." Because no matter what, she wasn't going to bullshit with him like nothing had happened between them. She simply wasn't wired that way. Yesterday she'd probably been too bitchy but he'd taken her off guard and they'd had somewhat of an audience. Today they were alone so she could be civil and grownup, but she still wanted answers from him.

He tugged his cap off as he fell in step with her. She was average in height but being next to him she always felt smaller. It was his shoulders more than anything. They were broad and muscular and she'd clutched onto them as he'd kissed a path down her jaw, neck and...nope. No, no, no. Not going there this morning. Too bad her nipples didn't get the memo. They tightened into hard buds as she remembered how he'd sucked and teased them while he brought her to climax with his very talented fingers.

"I screwed up," he blurted as they reached the front counter.

Not caring at all about the coffee, she stopped and turned to him. "Yes, you did." She crossed her arms over her chest, knowing it was a defensive gesture but unable to stop herself. The man put her on edge in more ways than one. Since moving to Holly she hadn't thought about dating or the opposite sex. Or for the last four years really. At least not in more than an abstract way. She could appreciate a sexy guy as much as the next woman but when she'd taken guardianship of her sister she'd been twenty-one. Dating or men hadn't even been on her radar—until Jackson.

He looked her right in the eye as he spoke. "I should have called and I'm sorry I didn't."

Jaw tight, she nodded. "Okay." As apologies went it was pretty lame, but she would accept it. And move on from him.

"I got...okay, this will sound like bullshit, but I got scared."

She dropped her arms, snorting in disbelief. "That does sound like garbage. You got *scared?*"

He scrubbed a hand over his head in a gesture she'd come to learn meant he was nervous. The action was rare from him. "Yeah."

Bullshit. "So you got scared...but still managed to take Angelia out a couple days after me." After he'd told her that he didn't want to be with anyone else. It wasn't as if they'd made promises to each other, not exactly. But she deserved more than a man who'd pursued her hard, hooked up with her, then just stopped calling. Damn it, she hadn't wanted to bring up Angelia, hadn't wanted him to know it had hurt her so badly.

Which just made the confusion on his face piss her off even more. "I didn't take her out."

Nora's lips pulled into a thin line. "Gossip in Holly spreads fast, Jackson. You know that more than most." He'd grown up here, unlike her, so he should definitely be aware.

"I don't care what you heard, I didn't take Angelia out." His expression darkened for a moment before understanding seemed to dawn in his gaze. "I took her home a few weeks ago when she got a flat and didn't have a spare, but that's it. Nothing's ever happened between us and never will."

She bit her bottom lip. He sounded as if he was telling the truth. He might have hurt her, but Nora had never taken him for a liar. "Okay, I believe you. It still doesn't explain what happened. Damn it, Jackson, we were friends."

"Were?"

She shrugged, the action jerky. "You know what I mean." When they'd become intimate they'd taken a step from friends to lovers. Or so she'd thought. Which was why it had cut so deep. They'd talked and texted every day for months. Then nothing. Like she didn't matter.

"I'm sorry, Nora. When we crossed that line it was, I don't know. I could see more happening with you."

"More?"

"More than just..." He cursed again. "I saw a future with you and it scared me."

MERRY CHRISTMAS, BABY | 23

She wasn't sure how to take that at all, but she knew she didn't like the knot in the pit of her stomach. "Why?"

"I've been single a long time. You knocked me on my ass when we met. Then when we got together, it was intense. I pussied out. There's no other excuse for it. But I want another chance, to start over with you."

"No." She held up a hand when he started to protest. "I like you Jackson, but no. We can be friends." She wasn't going to give him more than that. Because what happened when she let him back in and he got 'scared' again? No way. Her last real boyfriend had bailed when she'd gotten guardianship of Sasha.

His jaw tightened, the gleam in his eyes something she couldn't quite define. "Friends?"

She nodded. "We were friends before. We'll just pretend that little...date never happened." Even as she said it, her cheeks warmed up. Pretending she'd never felt his hands and mouth on her body was going to be very hard. She'd missed him so much; more than she would admit to anyone. She'd missed the way he made her feel just by being in the same room, the way he always made her smile, the way—

He took a small step forward, slightly crowding her against the glass counter. He didn't touch her, but placed his hands on either side of her, caging her in. A subtle, spicy masculine scent teased her nose, wrapping around her and making it difficult to think straight. That and the way he was looking down at her with unrestrained lust in his gaze. "You want me to pretend I've never kissed you, never seen those pretty pink nipples shiny from my kisses?"

His words sent a rush of heat through her, flooding between her legs with no warning. Her nipples tightened as well as she remembered him doing exactly that. She resisted the urge to squirm. "Yes." The word came out as a scratchy whisper.

He leaned a fraction closer. "Pretend I've never felt your slickness on my fingers and watched you come apart in my arms?"

Oh, God. His words set her on fire. She ached for him everywhere, the pulse between her legs wild and out of control. It was almost too much. Somehow she managed to nod, which was good, because she couldn't find her voice.

He watched her for a long moment, those intense eyes searching hers. For a second she thought he might kiss her. The weakest part of her considered letting him, but he just nodded and stepped back a few inches.

She immediately missed the warmth of him—and cursed herself for it. But at least she could breathe now that he'd given her space. It was as if all her surroundings came back in a rush; Jackson O'Connor was no longer her sole focus. It was like she'd completely forgotten where she was. This man was dangerous in so many ways. Even being friends with him was going to wreak havoc on her senses.

"Are you free tonight? To get together—as friends." The last word held a note of distaste.

A small part of her was disappointed that he was accepting just friendship so easily, but she knew it was for the best. "I can't. Sasha and I are going Christmas tree shopping."

He blinked, all lust fading to be replaced by shock. "You don't have a tree yet? Christmas is in—"

"Four days, I know." She threw up her hands in mock self-defense. "Sasha was crazy with school and I've been the same with work since she got out for winter break. It just got away from us. And in my defense, it's Christmas here year round. It's easy to lose track of time."

"I can meet you guys here, help you lug it home." The offer sounded innocent enough, but there as a glint of well, hunger, in his gaze as he said it.

"Look, Jackson—"

"As friends. Seriously. You're never going to be able to get a proper sized tree tied down on your car roof."

She hated that he was right. She'd been dreading trying to figure out how they'd even get a tree home. Since she lived downtown she'd thought about just dragging it. "If Sasha's fine with it, then okay."

"I, uh, saw her yesterday."

"She told me."

"She also tell you I dropped an F bomb?"

Nora's lips twitched. "Yeah but I wouldn't worry about it. I'm sure she's heard worse at school." The fact that he looked guilty about it, however, just served to melt her heart even more. Which only annoyed her. There would be no melting for Jackson O'Connor.

"Want me to meet you here after work?"

She nodded. "Yeah, I'm going to let one of the girls close up so five is good if it works for you." And if Sasha was fine with him coming.

"I'll be here at five unless you tell me otherwise."

"Okay."

When he left she ordered herself not to stare at him as he walked away but it was hard not to drink in the sight of him. Thick, muscular legs, a tight...gah. They were just going to be friends from now on.

Unfortunately she figured that was something she'd have to remind herself of more than once. And that pretty much sucked. She'd allowed herself to see a future with him, especially after he'd opened up to her, had told her that he wanted to be with her and no one else. Now...she shook her head. She wouldn't allow herself to go there. Not again.

CHAPTER THREE

Jackson cursed under his breath when he saw his mom
stepping out of Silver Bells. Her auburn hair fell right
below her shoulders and had clearly just been styled. He
loved his mother, but she was going to ask what he was
doing and if he told her the truth she'd offer advice about
courting Nora, as she put it.

Her blue eyes lit up when she saw him. "My favorite
son." Smiling, she pulled him into a tight hug.

"You say that to all of us," he murmured, laughing
against the top of her head. For such a petite woman she
had a firm grip. "Hair looks good."

Stepping back, she patted it lightly. "It does, doesn't
it? I heard you were in here yesterday buying flowers."

His lips quirked up. "Is there a question in there?"

"Don't be smart with me. And no, because I also heard
from Macy Baker that you gave them to Nora. Why haven't you invited that girl to our Christmas Eve dinner?"

"We're just friends." Unfortunately. His fault. "Besides I think she's going to the Winter Wonderland Festival."

"So? Invite her as your friend. She can come after the
festival. Half the town's going to be there. Oh, invite
Sasha too. I just love those girls. Best thing that ever happened to that shop was Nora taking over." She snorted

27

and flicked a glance down the semi-crowded sidewalk. "Doesn't even look like the same place anymore."

He nodded in agreement. An aunt, some distant relative of Nora's on her father's side, had left the place to her because she was the only family left. Before Nora had whipped it into shape the place had been a used bookstore in serious need of help. It had been the only eyesore on Main Street. "It's not."

"Oh, I heard through the grapevine that there are a few young men interested in Nora. Some have asked her out—and she's said yes. Thought you might want to know." Her tone was so mild she might as well have been talking about the weather. Before he could respond she'd turned on her heel, her long green coat billowing at the ends as she swiveled.

Jackson frowned as he continued down the sidewalk. Since his mom was just coming from the beauty shop there was no doubt she'd heard all the latest gossip of the week. And *young men* to his mom were guys his age. He couldn't blame anyone for being interested in Nora. She was beautiful, smart and sweet. Didn't mean he had to like it. He wanted to know who had asked her out, but knew that would be a bad idea to actually ask Nora. He had to play things right with her. He wouldn't win her affection by grilling her about potential dates.

"Jackson."

Blinking, he realized he'd reached Nora's shop and she was standing outside, bundled up in a thick black pea coat, crimson scarf and a red and white, knitted cap with candy canes on it. She half-smiled. "You okay?"

"Yeah." He'd just been lost in his thoughts—something that *never* happened to him. He had situational awareness at all times. It had been drilled into him in the Navy, specifically when he was with the SEALs. He could traverse any terrain on the planet, kill someone countless ways with his bare hands and can and had survived behind enemy lines with his team on more than one occasion. But the thought of Nora going out with someone else twisted him up. He could try to chalk it up to simple jealousy but it was more than that. "I like your cap."

"Sasha told me it was geeky."

He lifted his shoulders. "I like geeky." Or her brand of it. God, he adored everything about her. He'd never had a problem with women. Not talking to them and certainly not bedding them. With Nora, he seemed to lose most of his charm because it was too damn hard to think and breathe around her. Mainly because he knew that she was *it* for him. He'd known on one level that once they crossed the line from friends to lovers things would change, but after their date he'd realized that it was more than a simple change. He'd seen his bachelorhood completely wiped out. He was fine with that, wanted a future with Nora, but it had knocked his legs out from under him. Which was a lame excuse for why he'd stopped calling her, but there it was.

Her cheeks flushed pink; a delicious shade he'd seen her turn when he'd made her come. Something he shouldn't be thinking about right now. Too late to forget about it though. "Where's Sasha?"

"I was just about to call you. She cancelled because she wanted to hang out with friends instead." Nora smiled but it didn't reach her eyes.

Though she'd never say it, he knew that it likely hurt her. "She's seventeen."

"I know. God, am I that transparent? I'm glad she's made so many friends since we moved here. I was just looking forward to getting a tree today."

"I'm still game." Anything to hang out with Nora. He just loved being with her, and being alone with her was even better because it allowed him more time to show her that he was still the same guy he'd always been—and to win her over for good.

"You sure? Don't feel obligated—"

"I'll pretend you didn't say that. Come on." He slung an arm around her shoulders in a completely friendly manner. At least that was what he told himself. He just wanted to touch her, to hold her close—to claim her mouth so intently she never wanted to walk away from him. When she was pressed up against him, he always felt content in a way he'd never imagined. She simply fit with him; this was where she was supposed to be.

Thankfully she leaned into him. "You smell good."

"Yeah?" He'd just come from his woodworking shop.

"Like pine and some kind of oils."

"I finished up on my dad's new rocking chair." He'd been working on it for weeks.

"Is it a Christmas present?" she asked as they maneuvered around a woman walking three poodles—all of them wearing little Santa hats. Poor pooches.

"Yeah, been working on it the past few weeks." The instant the words were out of his mouth he felt her stiffen just the slightest fraction. If they'd been talking the last three weeks it was something he would have shared with her. God, he was such a freaking idiot. "I'm right here," he tacked on as they reached his truck. He'd managed to snag a spot right on Main Street.

She stepped out of his embrace and he felt the loss immediately. "This will be so much easier to get the tree back to my place. Thanks again."

He didn't audibly respond, just opened the passenger door for her. He didn't want her thanks, he just wanted her—in his bed and in his life with a ring on her finger. Yeah, it was too soon for the ring, but he knew himself well enough that she was it for him and the ring would come soon enough. When he made a decision, he rarely changed his mind. Nora was his. Now he just needed to convince her.

* * *

"Jackson O'Connor. You're not paying for that." Nora went to snatch the cash out of his hand but he did some sort of smooth sidestep thing—unapologetically blocking her—as he passed the cash over to Mr. Collins, the man who ran the local Christmas tree lot.

"You want me to help you load it up on the truck?" Mr. Collins asked, both the men completely ignoring her.

"Yeah, thanks," Jackson said.

She followed after them, not holding onto her steam very well. She couldn't exactly get mad that he'd paid for her tree, but it felt like too much for just a friend to do. Who was she kidding? She wanted more than friendship and knew he did too. And she only got whiplash thinking about that. She wanted to give him another chance, but...the hurt of the past few weeks was too fresh. She'd forgiven him, but she still felt raw.

Refusing to think about that right now, she watched his graceful movements as he hoisted up one end of the tree as if it weighed absolutely nothing. He was wearing his favorite beat-up leather jacket that looked as if it had been custom made for him. A bomber jacket, dark jeans and work boots apparently equaled the sexiest thing she'd ever seen on a man. Or at least on Jackson. She loved the way it smelled too. Like leather, wood, oils and something masculine that was all him.

Part of her hated that she'd felt his hands on her bare skin, stroking across her breasts, down her stomach and... Yeah, they were just friends all right. She nearly snorted at the thought. She missed his touch way too much for that to be true. And there had been nothing friendly about his teasing and kisses.

Once the men had tied the tree down to the bed of the truck she slid into the passenger seat. "Jackson, you didn't—"

"I wanted to," he said as he started the engine.

"Okay, then thank you. And I'll make you hot chocolate when we get back to my place. If you can stay?" She chose her words carefully because he'd just offered to help with the tree, nothing more.

"Yeah, I'd love to."

That shouldn't make her so happy, but knowing they'd get to spend more time together turned her inside out. She'd missed him so much these past few weeks. Settling into Holly had changed something inside her for the better. The people here were real and she finally felt like she'd come home. "I think Sasha is interested in a boy," she said as he turned down a side street. Her townhome was only about five blocks away.

He shot her a quick glance. "Who?"

"I don't know, that's the problem. She's been a little secretive lately and she's always been nuts about texting but in the past few weeks it's been out of control. And, it's a girl thing, but I can tell from her expressions when she's texting that it's someone she's into."

"She hasn't said anything?"

"No. And we've always shared everything with each other." Nora had had to tow the mother-sister line pretty carefully since becoming Sasha's official guardian. Though the truth was, she'd always been more of a mother than their own had been so slipping into the role hadn't been much of a stretch.

"You think that's who she's with today?"

"Maybe. I mean, I don't think she'd lie to me though."

Nora hoped not. They'd always been honest with each other and she'd made it clear that her sister could come to her about anything.

"Fallon never said anything when she was interested in someone. It's probably just a teenage girl thing."

Nora snorted. "Fallon probably didn't say anything because of her three older brothers."

Jackson's lips pulled up in a smile that melted Nora from the inside out. "Yeah, there's that too." He cleared his throat. "By the way, my mom wanted to know if you and Sasha were available on Christmas Eve. My parents do this big dinner party thing. No pressure though." The words came out in a rush, which was unlike him.

"Ah, I'll let you know." Christmas Eve dinner seemed like a big deal. She didn't know from personal experience considering her own mother had rarely done anything special for the holidays, but she'd always tried to do something fun for Sasha the last few years. Even if it was just the two of them. A big thing with Jackson's family sounded fun, if a little intimidating. Though she didn't know his brothers well, she adored his sister and mother. She'd planned on going to the local festival but she could do that first.

"I'd like you to come as well. In case that wasn't clear." The deep tone of his voice wrapped around her, making her lightheaded as it often did.

She simply nodded, unable to find her voice. What was she doing, thinking they could just be friends? The longer she was around him, the clearer it was that was pretty much an impossible feat. Thankfully they'd reached her place and apparently it was a Christmas miracle because there was parking in front of the townhome next to hers.

"If you get the door I'll get the tree."

"You're sure?" It was over six feet and pretty thick.

Jackson just gave her a look that said he couldn't believe she'd asked that question. And yeah, okay, it was clear he could get it by himself. That didn't mean she wanted him to have to. Anticipation hummed inside her as she headed for the door. She might have said they were just going to be friends, but soon they'd be hanging out alone. She wasn't sure she had the willpower to resist him, even to protect her heart.

* * *

Jackson lugged the tree into Nora's place, ready to move 'Operation Win Nora Over' into full effect. If Sasha was out with friends, now was the perfect opportunity. "It smells like Christmas in here already," he said, moving past the entryway into the foyer.

She let out a light laugh and motioned to a glass bowl on the small table by the front door. "I sprayed the decorative pinecones with cinnamon oil."

36 | KATIE REUS

"Where to?"

"Living room. I've already got a place ready." She held out a hand, motioning to the room right off the foyer.

Careful with the blue spruce tree, he maneuvered it inside. Two gold and red throws were draped over her couches, stockings were up on the faux fireplace mantel and a stack of shiny presents were next to the window nook. She already had a gold tree skirt and stand laid out.

"I'll take this end while you maneuver the bottom in," she said, moving up beside him. Her sweet vanilla scent teased him. Even with the Christmas scents permeating the air, he could pick out her scent anywhere. It was subtle and all Nora—and made him crazy.

"Sounds good." It only took a few minutes until they had the tree in place and screwed in tight. He'd sensed her softening at the tree lot and on the way back to her place. He wasn't sure how much yet, but the attraction between them was still there full force. It was one hurdle he didn't have to worry about.

When he pushed up from his crouching position Nora was tugging her scarf and cap off. Her dark hair was slightly mussed and her cheeks were a perfect shade of pink to give him wicked, wicked thoughts about taking her mouth in a demanding, hungry kiss. At that thought his jeans started to get too tight so he cleared his throat. "I think I remember something about hot chocolate."

Laughing, she tilted her head toward the kitchen. Yeah, this was the Nora he'd fallen for. "Come on."

"How is it you never visited Holly before taking over your aunt's shop?" She'd been evasive when he'd asked her that months ago but he was still curious. Hell, he wanted to know everything about Nora.

She shrugged slightly, the action jerky as she pulled down a couple mugs from one of the cabinets. He sat at the center island, watching her movements, drinking in every line and curve of her tight body. She'd taken her coat off too and her dark jeans were snug and showed off her perfect ass. Yeah, staring at her like that wasn't helping the fit of his jeans either.

"She was my father's aunt and after he split, my mom didn't want anything to do with his side of the family. I didn't find out until after she died, but I guess Aunt Tammy had reached out to her multiple times over the years, but my mom..." She let out a sigh, shook her head. "She was an unhappy woman."

It was hard to picture that when Nora was the opposite. "Because your dad left?"

"I honestly don't know. He left right after Sasha was born and I remember them fighting a lot before then but I don't...I was eight, I just don't know. I only ever remember my mom being sad." There was a touch of the same emotion in her voice as she spoke. "She was never officially diagnosed but I think she was depressed most of her life."

"I'm sorry," he murmured.

"Thanks. The cancer was hard to deal with." She pulled a bar of chocolate from another cabinet. "And I've never said this out loud to anyone..." She glanced over her shoulder, gave him an assessing look.

"What?"

"I feel bad saying this, but...when she died, it was like a huge weight had been lifted. I'm still sad she's gone, but the emotional burden of taking care of her and Sasha had been draining. And she wasn't the best mother." The words came out in a rush, as if she didn't want to say them at all.

Jackson was glad she was opening up. They'd been flirty and friendly over the last six months but this was more real and what he wanted from her. If she was telling him this, she at least trusted him. "I can imagine."

"God, I hope not. Your mom is like Mary Poppins, I swear. I..." Trailing off, she cleared her throat and set a pot on the stove. "So tell me about this big Christmas shindig."

He wanted to dig more into her past, but didn't want to push too hard, too fast. "My mom's obsessed with Christmas—like most of the town. So she invites half the town."

Nora adjusted the pot on the stove and turned to face him. "Really?"

"Nah, it just feels like it. That first Christmas back was hard." The words were out of his mouth before he could think about censoring himself. But if she was going to open up to him, he wanted to be more honest with her.

"You mean after you got out of the Navy?"

He nodded, glad she understood him. "Yeah. I didn't think I'd have trouble adjusting to civilian life, but..." He shrugged. It had been a hell of a lot more difficult than he'd imagined. Adjusting to the crowds and more than that, dealing with civilians. It had been hard to care about seemingly trivial things when Americans were losing their lives overseas. That battle had been the hardest to get over and some days he still struggled with it. Not as much anymore since the whole reason he'd volunteered was to protect his country.

In a move that was completely Nora's style, she crossed the small kitchen and laid her hand over his. "I'm sorry. I can't even imagine how hard it would be to come back from...all that. And then settle in with any sense of normalcy."

Somehow he thought Nora could imagine it just fine. She was a fighter in her own right. It sounded as if she'd been raising her sister since she was eight years old. He slid his other hand over hers, the need to touch her overwhelming. Even before they'd kissed, before that first date, he'd made excuses to touch her all the damn time. Over the summer it had been even worse because she loved flirty summer dresses. And she wore the type reminiscent of the fifties; retro, she'd told him they were called. Whatever they were, they showed off sleek toned legs he'd fantasized about for far too long.

When his hand settled in place, he saw her eyes dilate. The pulse point in her neck beat wild and out of control and her breathing increased just a fraction. He wanted to lean in, to capture her mouth with his. She'd let him too, he could see it in her eyes. But he wasn't sure if she was just having a weak moment and he didn't want to take advantage—and give her a reason to regret kissing him later.

Being just friends was never going to work for them. Not since they'd gotten a taste of each other. That first taste wasn't nearly enough though. Something told him it would never be enough. That was fine though, he was going to take things slowly, do things right with her.

A soft buzzing sound filled the air and it took a second for it to register it was her phone vibrating across the counter. She blinked and withdrew her hand from his, breaking the spell. Immediately he missed the warmth, her softness.

When she looked at the screen her expression paled. "It's my security company for the store. The alarm must have gone off."

Which meant someone had likely broken into her store.

CHAPTER FOUR

"Jackson, you don't need to go with me." Nora looped her scarf around her neck and tucked her gloves into her jacket pocket. She wasn't exactly scared, but she wasn't looking forward to dealing with the aftermath of a break-in—if there even was one.

He snorted, as if she'd lost her mind. "Your car's still down by your shop."

"Yeah, and I can walk." She lived downtown so it wasn't too far. Plus the cops would be there.

"It's after dark."

"Holly is one of the safest towns in probably the world."

"And your shop was just broken into."

"We don't know that." She'd just gotten a call from her security company that the alarm had been triggered, but didn't know anything beyond that. "And the sheriff's department has already been alerted so I'll be fine."

"The longer you argue with me, the longer you waste time. We could be there by now." When she started to respond, he cut her off. "And if you try to walk on your own, I'll just follow in my truck."

Nora saw the determined set to his jaw and the tight line of his shoulders. "I never knew you were this stubborn." It shouldn't be so sexy. But apparently everything about him was, at least to her—and any woman with a pulse.

He nodded once. "I am when it comes to someone I care about."

Okay then. She cared about him too, but... she wasn't going there right now. She was still rattled from their almost-kiss in the kitchen. Maybe he hadn't intended to kiss her, but the sparks had been there, at least for her. And she'd felt herself falling, falling, falling. She'd been ready to lean into that kiss, into him, and lose control in a way she'd sworn to herself she wouldn't again. "Well I can't exactly argue with that," she murmured, grabbing her keys from the hook by the door.

He gave her a look of pure satisfaction that reminded her a lot of the way he'd looked after he'd made her climax. Nope, not going there either.

As she slid into the front seat of his truck she pulled her cell out. "I'm going to call Sasha just to check on her." The call from the alarm company probably shouldn't rattle her so much, but it was instinct to check on her sister. Didn't matter that they lived in a safe town, bad things happened every day, everywhere. And okay, she was being totally paranoid. But she wouldn't apologize for it.

Jackson turned down the radio as she called, the thoughtful action not lost on her.

"Hey," Sasha answered after the third right, slightly out of breath.

"Hey yourself. You doing okay?"

"Uh, yeah." She let out a short laugh. "Why, what's up?"

"Nothing, just checking on you. Got the tree set up."

"We can decorate in the morning if you want," Sasha said, excitement in her voice.

The excitement meant way too much to Nora. She wanted her sister to have the best Christmas this year. Things felt somehow different since settling in Holly. More permanent. Now that she'd heard Sasha's voice most of her worry dissipated. If her store had been broken into, yes, it would be a pain in the butt to deal with, but her sister was okay. That was what really mattered. Nora had just needed to hear her voice.

"Sounds good to me. I want to grab a few things from Carol's place tomorrow." Her friend Carol ran Christmas Carol's Shop & Crafts and had wreath making kits. Nora was going to try her hand at making one. The good thing about living in Holly was, she could use the wreath year round.

"Okay. Listen...I wanted to stay over at Liz's house tonight if that's okay?"

She was out for winter break and Liz was a good kid. "Okay, put her mom on the phone, I want to talk to her first."

"Ah, hold on..." There was a slight rustling in the background, then Sasha came over the line. "She's at a Christmas thing with Liz's dad."

"Unless I talk to her mom, you're not staying over there."

"They won't be back 'til after midnight." Sasha's voice bordered on whiny, which was unlike her.

"Then you should have thought about it sooner. Listen, I'm pulling up to the shop so unless I hear from her mom directly I expect to see you home by your curfew."

"Why are you at the shop?"

"Ah, it's no big deal, but I just got a call from the security company." She decided to downplay it until she knew more. No need to make her sister worry. "I see the sheriff. I've gotta go but I'll see you later tonight." The flashing blue lights of his car reflected off the big glass windows of her shop and the neighboring ones. The sight of a police car against the backdrop of Main Street with its vintage light poles and pretty sparkling twinkle lights lining the street seemed out of place.

"The sheriff?" There was a note of panic in Sasha's voice.

"Oh, it's nothing to worry about. Just a glitch." She hoped—and she certainly wasn't going to worry her sister. This wasn't something Sasha needed to think about. "I'll call you later."

"That was some nice parenting," Jackson murmured as she ended the call.

She laughed. "I try. There's Brad." Nora was glad it was the sheriff and not one of his officers. Not that she had anything against them, but she was comfortable with him. He came into her coffee shop at least twice a week.

"Brad?" There was a strange note to Jackson's voice as he parked his truck along the curb behind a four-door sedan.

"Yeah, Sheriff Fulton. He grew up here, I thought you'd know him." Jackson couldn't be more than a year or two older than him.

"I do." Everything about Jackson's posture was stiff.

She wanted to ask him about it, but couldn't dwell on it. Not when she had to deal with whatever had happened at her shop. An icy blast of air rolled over her as she stepped out onto the curb. She'd barely taken a step before Jackson was at her side, his arm around her shoulders. She leaned into his warmth as they headed for the sheriff's car. Even though she'd protested his coming with her, she was grateful he'd pushed. It was nice to have someone to depend on.

Brad nodded at both of them, his expression polite and professional as usual. Broad and muscular, he was probably about six feet even if she had to guess. She'd heard that he had a bunch of medals from his time in the Marine Corps and had literally saved a drowning puppy once. He was an All-American hero and he certainly looked the part in his pressed uniform.

"The alarm's gone off and two of my guys are inside already."

Worry punched through her as she glanced at the front doors. She'd been trying to keep it at bay but couldn't now that she was here. Neither the entrance to the coffee shop nor the bookstore should have been open. And she didn't see any broken glass from the doors or windows. "How did they get in?"

"Back door was unlocked."

"Unlocked or open?" Jackson asked before she could speak.

"Just unlocked." He turned his focus back to her. "We're going to need you to do an inventory, see if anything was taken or broken before you make a report."

She nodded, fighting the tension racing up her spine. "I can make some coffee for you and your guys before I start."

"I'll do it," Jackson murmured, kissing the top of her head in a way she could only define as completely, and utterly possessive. Especially considering the pointed look he shot Brad after he did it.

It was so blatantly, well, possessive was pretty much the only way to describe it. And she liked it a little bit too much.

* * *

"So far nothing seems to be missing," Brad said as Jackson slid him a mug of coffee across the counter.

Nora had already gone through the coffee shop and was now in the bookstore, meticulously going through everything. Jackson wanted to be with her, but knew she needed to focus and he'd just be a distraction. "Yeah. It's a little weird." He didn't like it. "Have there been any break-ins around here lately?"

The sheriff shook his head. "No. Few residential things but we know who did it."

"Teenagers?"

"Yep." He shot Jackson an assessing look. "When are you going to man up and make things official with Nora?"

Jackson's fingers froze around his own mug. "What the hell are you talking about?"

Lips twitching, Brad just lifted a shoulder. "There's a bet going at Silver Bells. Just curious is all, especially considering the 'stay away from my woman or die' look you gave me outside."

"What the fu—"

"Hey, your mom started the bet." He gave another shrug.

"My mother started a bet on *what* exactly?"

"Not sure what the actual term that she used was, but as soon as Nora's officially your girlfriend, the winner gets a pretty big pot."

His gaze narrowed. "How big?"

"I think it's up to six hundred bucks. Plus they win a gift certificate to the spa and a free salon day at Silver Bells. The works."

"My mother's insane."

"I think that's up for debate."

"You're just saying that because she brings you cookies all the time." His mom was absolutely shameless.

"There might be some truth in that." His lips quirked again before he took a sip of the coffee. "Man, Nora's got the best brew in town, I swear."

Something about the way Brad said Nora's name ran-
kled Jackson. It was too familiar. He hadn't even realized
they were friends. "You ever ask her out?"

Now the sheriff full-on smiled. "God, you are so done.
And no, not that I didn't think about it." When Jackson
just scowled Brad's smile grew even wider. "But she
never gave me the vibe and you put a claim on her pretty
early on. Not that you've ever done anything about it."
He cleared his throat. "Never thought SEALs were cow-
ards."

"Shut it, jarhead." Fulton had been a year behind Jackson in school, had gone on to join the Marine Corps and
after doing four years—almost the entire time overseas—
got out and earned a degree in criminal justice before
settling back in Holly. And Jackson knew the guy had
some notable medals that he never talked about.

Shaking his head slightly, he slid his mug back to
Jackson. "Top it off?"

Nodding, he did. As he grabbed the pot, Fulton continued. "You know of any issues Nora's had lately? Any
enemies, anything like that?"

"No and she would have told me." Or he assumed she
would have. He couldn't imagine anyone having anything against Nora anyway. There'd been no destruction
of property either. So far it looked as if her back door had
been opened after the alarm had been set, which set it
off.

"I figured as much. Gonna head down to talk to the employee who closed up after this, but this doesn't feel like a break-in."

It didn't, but Jackson still didn't like it. When another thought occurred, he frowned. "What date did my mom pick?"

"Christmas Eve."

He sighed. Yeah, that sounded about right.

* * *

"I'm glad that's over." Nora wrapped her arms around herself, fighting off a shiver as they watched Brad and his officers drive off. They'd gotten a few curious onlookers headed to Yuletide Spirits earlier, but luckily not too many people had stopped to talk.

Wouldn't really matter though. By tomorrow it would be all over town that she'd had the cops at her store tonight. Which was actually a good thing. She'd get even more foot traffic during the day from curious people and she'd do even more business. A win-win as far as she was concerned.

"Me too." Jackson's deep voice rolled over her.

It was like her body was attuned to him. Whenever he spoke in that dark, delicious way, everything inside her seemed to wake up and take notice without fail. Well that and being around him in general. After the way he'd helped with her tree, then stayed at the shop while she dealt with the tedious job of checking out everything, she couldn't help but question the decision she'd made to keep things platonic between them. The fact was, they had chemistry and he was such a sweet man. There was no getting around it. But...gah, she was such a coward. She'd had enough loss in her life, she didn't want to lose Jackson too.

"You feel like heading home or you want to grab a drink? I'm not sure if there's a live band at Yuletide's tonight, but they'll have good music regardless."

She started to glance at her phone but then nodded. Screw it. Sasha was on holiday break and Nora didn't need to be home for a while yet. And she really wanted to spend time with Jackson, even if she was unsure if she wanted to give things a shot with him. She hooked her arm through his. "Yuletide's."

Right off Main Street and Mistletoe Avenue, it was the perfect place to relax.

"What's your curfew tonight?" Jackson murmured as they reached the main door. The glint in his eyes was pure wicked hunger.

Somehow she found her voice. "I don't have one." She trusted her sister to get home in time so if she was a little late, well, she was freaking twenty-five years old. She'd just be late.

"Good."

When he opened the door, an energetic song filtered out. No live band tonight but the place was packed with customers three-deep at the long, mahogany bar. Bottles upon bottles were stacked behind it.

"I don't know if we'll even be able to find—" She stopped when she saw Carol Cardini waving at them from a high-top table. And there were two empty chairs there. Even if she was waiting for someone, Nora and Jackson could join her for a few minutes. At least long enough to grab a drink. When Carol pointed to the empty seats, Nora smiled and nodded.

"That woman is always happy, I swear," Jackson said, barely loud enough for her to hear.

He wasn't wrong. Tall, blonde and on a scale of one to ten, she was fifteen on the gorgeous meter. No surprise she had on a red, formfitting dress—her favorite color. With killer curves, it would be easy to dislike the bombshell on principle, especially since she would have given Marilyn Monroe a run for her money, but Carol was so damn sweet. And she always had a bright smile on her face. Lately though, Nora thought she looked a little sad and distracted, no matter the put-together picture she portrayed. She knew Carol's mom had been mayor, but then had gotten sick. That was before Nora had moved to town though so she didn't know all the details.

"Jackson!" A familiar and slightly annoying female voice drew both their attention as they made their way through the throng of high-top tables.

Nora turned to find Angelia sliding up to him in a skintight, shimmery silver dress, even though he had his arm around Nora.

Completely ignoring Nora, the pretty blonde gave him a hug and kissed him on the cheek noisily. If he hadn't turned his head at the last minute she'd have gotten his mouth. The thought of another woman's lips on Jackson's made imaginary claws flare up inside Nora. She hadn't realized she could actually feel that jealous of another person, but damn. "I've gotta run, but thanks for the ride home the other night." The way she said 'ride', there was no mistaking the innuendo of what she really meant.

The words were a slam to Nora's senses. She'd believed Jackson when he told her that nothing had happened between him and Angelia. Still, there was a tiny, lingering doubt in the back of her mind. She'd never taken Jackson for a liar, but she'd been fooled before. Her last serious boyfriend had dumped her when she got guardianship of her sister. He hadn't wanted a ready-made family. Given how young they'd been she hadn't exactly blamed him. It had cut deeply though since she'd never pegged him for being so cold and callous. Then he'd pulled the rug out from under her.

It was hard not to wonder if she was wrong about Jackson too.

CHAPTER FIVE

"Are you freaking kidding me?" Nora muttered to herself as she glanced around the bookstore. After closing up and heading out with Jackson and the police last night she'd been extra conscious of where everything was. She'd even snapped some pictures with her phone. After she double checked the photos on her phone with the actual window nook in her shop, sure enough the pillows had been moved around.

Nora had taken the pictures once everyone was out of the shop, so there was no chance one of the officers had moved the pillows by accident. She didn't like knowing someone had been in here, someone who must have the security code. Well, they would have to because she'd reset it after she'd left. At least it narrowed down her suspect pool to three people. Frowning, she bent to adjust the pillows when a bright red scrap of material caught her eye. Tugging it out from under one of the pillows, her eyes widened when she saw it was a bra.

Oh, Lord. Was one of her employees in here doing...whatever with someone? She rubbed the bridge of her nose. At least someone was getting some action. Tucking the bra under her arm, she headed back to the coffee shop side and pulled out her phone to text Jackson. They hadn't stayed at Yuletide's long last night and

she was still feeling weird about that run-in with Angelia. Jackson had assured her that nothing had ever happened between them, but doubt edged its way in.

*Think I solved the break-in mystery. Found a bra tucked
in the pillows at work. Someone was in here after we left. They
must have the code. Gonna talk to everyone after Christmas,
figure out what's going on.* She could call an employee
meeting today with the ones who had the code but tomorrow was Christmas Eve and she closed up early. And
they weren't open at all on Christmas so, yeah, calling a
meeting like this could wait.

You need better security.

My security's fine.

There was a pause and she could practically hear his
snort of derision. *What time do you close today?*

Six. She was closing a little early today too.

*I'll be there at six sharp. We're going to set up a sting oper-
ation.*

She laughed out loud as she turned her OPEN sign
over and unlocked the door. *I can't tell if you're kidding.*

*Not joking. We'll set up a camera and can watch the feed
on your laptop. You owe me hot chocolate anyway. We can do
it tonight if you're free.*

She wanted to say no, but Sasha had already begged
her to stay over at Liz's house tonight since she hadn't
been able to last night. Nora thought they'd get to decorate the tree tonight at least—since Sasha had slept in this
morning they hadn't gotten to yet. But Sasha was such a
good kid and if she wanted to hang out with her friend,

Nora wasn't going to stop her. Her sister had lost a good portion of her childhood because of their mother.

Her fingers flew across the screen's keyboard. *This feels over the top but I'm curious so okay. You want to help me decorate my tree?*

Yes. I have an extra present for your tree too. See you at six.

He'd gotten her a present? Her heart started doing that crazy pitter patter again, kicking up a billion notches. She'd actually gotten him something too, weeks ago before their first and last date. She wasn't sure how to respond and was luckily saved by the little jingle of her front door.

Or so she thought until she looked up to see petite, pretty Angelia striding into her shop. She wore dark pants, boots and a thick jacket and scarf. What was up with this woman? And why did she have to show up before anyone else? Nora didn't know much about her other than she worked for one of the local real estate companies, and that she apparently had a thing for Jackson.

"Hey, Nora." She slid her sunglasses back on her head. "You're here bright and early. Smells good."

"Thanks. Do you know what you want or do you need a few minutes?"

"Yeah. Latte with non-fat milk, sugar free syrup and no whip. Sixteen ounce."

"One skinny latte coming up." Thankful to be busy with her hands, she turned back to her work station.

"So, you and Jackson huh?"

As she readied the espresso machine, Nora just smiled over her shoulder and made a noncommittal sound.

"Look, the reason I stopped by is because I feel bad. I didn't know you guys were together. If I had I never would have hooked up with him a couple weeks ago."

At the woman's words, everything inside Nora went still. She knew Jackson, not this woman. And deep down, it was too hard to believe he'd flat-out lied to her. But she suspected Angelia was. She gave a casual shrug as she turned back with the drink. "Okay. I put this in a to-go cup but I should have asked. Did you want to sit?"

"Uh, to-go is fine. Do you want to talk?" The words came out stilted, the previously confident woman looking completely unsure.

Not even a little bit. "We're good, no worries." She gave her best "shopkeeper smile" and rattled off the amount. She wanted the woman out of her shop.

Angelia blinked in surprise but pulled out a bill from her purse.

After making change she slid it across the counter. "Hope you have a great Christmas." Nora couldn't hide the fakeness from her voice no matter how hard she tried. Which wasn't very much.

Once the woman was gone, she let out a sigh of relief. She knew herself well enough that she'd ask Jackson about this, but she wasn't going to let jealousy eat her up inside. Heck, they weren't even together. They were just friends.

Keep telling yourself that, maybe you'll start to believe it, she thought.

* * *

"You don't think four cameras are overkill?" Hands on her hips, Nora looked up at Jackson who was on a ladder, hiding the last camera on the top of one of her bookshelves. They all had a wireless connection and some other specs he'd outlined—and sounded impressed with.

"Nope." He'd been completely focused since he arrived. They'd had to wait an extra fifteen minutes for some straggler customers, but as soon as they'd been alone he'd gone into what she considered his work mode.

It was a little intense. She'd shown up at his workshop early months ago and had seen him show the same sort of intensity when working on a project. He'd acknowledged her, but hadn't done much other than that. It was the same now. She wasn't sure why, but that sort of intensity on him was sexy, especially since she kept imagining him showing it in a very different setting.

"I can see why you were a good SEAL," she murmured.

That caught his attention. He looked down at her, gave her that trademark wicked grin. "I've never left a mission unfinished."

"This is a mission?"

"Yep." He was back to ignoring her as he finished situating the camera into place. When he was clearly satisfied his 'mission' was complete, he let out a grunt that could have meant anything before descending the steps. "Oh, my God, you look like a kid on Christmas morning. You're seriously excited about this?"

"Hell yeah. We're going to bust whoever this is."

"This is an interesting side to you." She didn't bother fighting her grin. It had to be one of her employees with the code but she still wanted to know who it was. Right now she just couldn't imagine any of them coming in here for some sort of liaison.

"Come on, let me check the laptop, see if all the feeds are coming through." As he moved to the counter in the bookshop, she decided to just ask what had been on her mind all day.

It didn't matter that she'd tried to ignore that little conversation with Angelia from earlier, it had kept replaying in her mind all freaking day. "Angelia stopped by my shop today."

He barely glanced at her, nodded as he typed commands into the keyboard. "Oh."

"She said she was sorry she hooked up with you a few weeks ago and that she wouldn't have if she'd know you and I were together." Which they weren't, but that wasn't the point.

"Oh...wait, what the hell?" He straightened, all his focus on her now. Raw indignation played across his features. "She said that?"

Nora nodded, a frisson of relief sliding through her veins at his reaction. "Yeah. I don't know her at all and I didn't really believe her but I wanted to tell you." And okay, ask him if it was true. She didn't need to ask him though, not now. The truth was written all over his face.

"I haven't touched another woman since we met."

She blinked. "Since our date or since we met?"

"Met."

Oh. Hell. She did *not* know how to respond to that. At all. Jackson was a gorgeous man, that being an understatement. Everything about him screamed raw sex appeal. And the way he was looking at her now, as if he was a predator about to pounce, had her completely melting. She wanted to step closer, wrap her arms around him and—Gah, not right now. Clearing her throat, she glanced at the computer, breaking his gaze. "We, uh, should probably check the laptop then get out of here."

She could feel his gaze on her, scorching hot. But she was apparently feeling extra cowardly because she refused to look at him. Too many emotions slammed through her at that revelation. And she just couldn't deal with how it made her feel. It was hard to believe that he hadn't been with anyone since meeting her, but that knowledge warmed her from the inside out. She just needed to figure out what she wanted to do about it. Well, the truth was, she wanted to see where things went with them. She'd been fantasizing about the sexy man for way too long.

After what felt like an eternity he turned back to the computer. "Feeds are working," he murmured after a few minutes, pinning her with his gaze again. "Let's get out of here. I've been thinking about that hot chocolate all day."

The look in his eyes told her he'd been thinking about more than hot chocolate. Way more. So had she. She was pretty sure she was done just thinking about it. Every time she looked at him, she remembered the way he'd stroked her to orgasm, the way his expert fingers had slid inside her, teasing and gentle… Just like that her body heated up and she felt her cheeks warm. Yep, it was definitely time to move on from the "just friends" category.

* * *

"I can't believe you've never seen A Christmas Story." Jackson had his arm stretched out across the back of the couch as she set their two mugs on the side table next to him.

"Then I'm glad I'm about to remedy that." Ignoring that little voice in the back of her head that told her she was asking for heartbreak, she sat next to him and curled into his side. She wasn't going to flat out jump him, but she'd come to realize that they would likely never be *just* friends. Not with the sizzling chemistry between them.

Jackson's only reaction was the slightest jolt so imperceptible she wouldn't have felt it if she hadn't been tucked up against him. His arm dropped from the top of the couch and curled around her shoulders, holding her in a loose enough embrace. That subtle, spicy scent that always drove her crazy teased her as the previews started. They had the laptop set up on the loveseat and so far, nothing exciting had happened at her shop. Which was just as well. Every second that passed she was finding it harder to care about anything but what it would feel like to have Jackson in her bed.

"You want me to pick you up tomorrow?" he murmured, his deep voice sending little shock waves across her senses.

His voice shouldn't affect her so much. "No, but thanks. I was going to bring her a bottle of wine or some dark chocolate truffles from Holly Jolly Chocolatier, but should I bring something else?"

"Just yourself." His voice had taken on a different tone, his grip tightening ever so slightly. They'd decorated her tree with lights and two boxes of ornaments when they'd first arrived and the sparkly white lights reflected off the television.

Not that she was really focused on anything else other than Jackson. Being held by him like this, all she could focus on was his strong embrace and the crazy way he made her feel. Her skin felt too tight for her body. She wanted to strip off his shirt and jeans and do the same with her own clothing so she could feel him skin to skin.

After a few minutes the arousal was so intense she couldn't ignore it. "Jackson..." She looked up to find his gaze hot, intense and completely on her. He didn't seem to care about the movie either.

Before she could think about the consequences of their actions—other than blinding pleasure—he grabbed her hips and tugged her so that she straddled him.

She braced herself against his shoulders and sank down completely over him, savoring the feel of having him between her legs like this. She was done fighting these feelings. It would suck if she got hurt, but if she never gave into this temptation, she'd never know what they might have. The truth was, the thought of him with someone else while they just remained friends shredded her up in ways she'd never imagined.

Jackson let out a groan as he grabbed her by the back of the head in a completely dominating grip. He met her half way and pulled her down to him, his mouth hungry and insistent. When his tongue demanded entrance into her mouth, she moaned into him, meeting him stroke for stroke. It was like her body had a mind of its own as she rolled her hips against him.

His erection was thick and insistent even through his jeans. She wanted to feel it inside her, wanted to be completely taken by him. Her nipples pebbled tightly against her bra cups as his hips jerked once, his arousal something she couldn't ignore.

Jackson tore his mouth from hers, his blue eyes bright with hunger as he stared up at her. "Want to see more of you," he rasped out, his breathing as erratic as her heartbeat.

She nodded, her heart rate out of control. She wanted to see more of him too—all of him. When she started to reach for the hem of his shirt, he froze.

"Damn it." The sudden curse made her fingers freeze on his shirt.

"You don't want—"

He tilted his head at the laptop. "Someone's in your shop."

The most insane part of her brain wanted to just keep doing what they were doing. To strip off the rest of their clothes and— "We've gotta go, huh?" Because if he said no—

He groaned and pressed his forehead to hers. "I think I might kill whoever's in there."

Forcing her muscles to work, she slid off him. The pulsing ache between her legs was even more insistent now. Now that her body knew she wasn't getting any more from Jackson, it wanted him even more badly. "I think I might help."

Suddenly he gripped the back of her neck again in that purely dominating way that made her melt. "We're finishing this when we get back." His voice was a low, raspy growl.

Unable to find her voice, she simply nodded. Oh yeah, they were definitely finishing this.

CHAPTER SIX

Jackson kept his weapon tucked in the back of his pants with his leather jacket covering it. He had a license to carry and used it more often than not. Just because he'd gotten out of the Navy didn't mean he'd lost all his survival instincts. Tonight, however, he wasn't going to need it. Not after who they'd just seen on Nora's laptop.

"She's so freaking dead," Nora muttered as they entered the storeroom of her shop. It was dimly lit but there was more than enough room to see everything.

The storeroom was split into two sections. This half was filled with open boxes of books and neatly stacked books ready to be stocked when necessary. It was all very organized, just like Nora.

"How do you want to do this?" he asked as he shut and locked the door behind him.

"Just...ugh, I don't know. I'll go in and figure out what she's doing here. Do you mind waiting in the storeroom?"

He shook his head and brushed his lips over hers. Nora's eyes widened slightly, but then just as quickly her cheeks flushed pink. They weren't going back to friends. Ever. Nora was it for him and after tonight, it was pretty clear that she wanted to be more than friends too. Hell, he'd known that for a while.

Sighing, she opened the door from the storeroom to the shop. When he heard a male voice, Jackson grabbed her upper arm out of instinct and tugged her back. She let out a soft gasp, but he ignored it and moved into the shop. A ten foot high bookshelf was to his left and a display of Christmas books and other Christmas items to his right. The soft murmur of a male voice filled the air. It carried enough that he guessed it was coming from the front of the store. The counter and too many displays blocked him from seeing for certain.

All of Jackson's instincts went on alert. They'd seen Sasha on the screen, but she'd been alone. If someone else was here, no way in hell was he letting Nora go in by herself. He started to reach for his weapon but then he recognized the voice.

Turning to look at Nora, he motioned to the line of light switches on the wall, then pointed to the shop. She knew how the light system worked better than him. "The front area," he whispered.

She nodded and flipped them. As soon as she did, he heard a female yelp of surprise. Without pausing, he strode forward with Nora right behind him. Sidestepping the counter and moving around the displays, he stopped at the front nook to find Sasha buttoning up her sweater and his own freaking cousin moving to step in front of her.

"What the heck is going on?" Nora demanded before anyone could speak.

Sasha's face was as crimson as her sweater as she stepped out from behind Donovan, who'd just turned eighteen. "Hey, Nora, I uh…" She cleared her throat and Donovan held out a hand for Nora after giving Jackson a wary look. "I'm Donovan O'Connor. I'm your sister's boyfriend. And Jackson's cousin."

"Boyfriend?" Sasha blurted.

Donovan turned before Nora could respond or attempt to shake his hand. "Are you seeing someone else?" he demanded.

"No, I just thought…"

"I'm not hiding us anymore, Sasha. I'm barely one year older than you. It's not illegal for us to be together. I care about you and I don't want to be with anyone else."

Jackson scrubbed a hand over his face. He so did not need to hear any of this.

Nora cleared her throat. "So, Sasha's boyfriend? Is there a reason you two have been sneaking around here? And why aren't you at Liz's house?"

Sasha looked mortified as she wrapped her arms around herself. "Her parents are heavy sleepers. I was planning on staying there, I swear, I just wanted some time alone with Donovan." She looked at the kid then, her expression softening to one of complete adoration.

Donovan looked just as smitten. Freaking puppy love.

"And you thought using my store was okay for that? You thought lying to me was okay? I'm assuming it was you who set off the alarm the other night?" Nora sounded more hurt than angry, her voice cracking on the last word. Jackson wanted to reach out and put his arm around her, but he could tell she needed to hash this out with her sister.

Sasha nodded. "Yeah," she whispered. "I'm really sorry. When you told me the cops showed up I should have said something but I thought you'd be pissed. We didn't touch anything and I punched the wrong code in when trying to enter, that's all. I was just distracted and..." Her cheeks flushed even deeper and Donovan actually looked embarrassed then.

Wasn't hard to guess why she'd put the wrong code in if Donovan had been distracting her. Oh, sweet Lord. By the panicked look on Nora's face she'd come to the same conclusion. Yeah, this was not the type of conversation the sisters needed to have in front of Jackson or Donovan.

"You drive here?" he asked his cousin.

"Yeah."

"I'm going to follow you home."

"Dude, that's not—"

"Yeah, it's freaking necessary and it's happening. We're leaving *now.*" He turned to Nora and not caring about their audience, he cupped her cheek. "See you tomorrow night?"

"Yeah." Her voice was soft, breathy and all he could envision was the way she'd straddled him on her couch barely twenty minutes before.

He should wring his cousin's neck for the interruption. He pressed his lips to Nora's, just a brief brush to reinforce his claim on her. Because she was his, no doubt about it. It took willpower he didn't know he had to pull back. But he wasn't starting something he couldn't finish. Nodding tightly, since he couldn't find his voice, he looked at his cousin and jerked his chin toward the back door.

"I'll call you later," Donovan murmured to Sasha before falling in step with Jackson.

Nora watched as Jackson left, thankful he'd taken the boy with him. Well, more like a man than a boy. God, when had her sister grown up so much? This was definitely new parenting territory and she wasn't sure she was ready for it. Not that she really had a choice.

"You want some chocolate cake?" she asked quietly. Chocolate pretty much fixed everything.

Sasha blinked and to Nora's surprise nodded as tears filled her eyes. "I'm sorry for lying."

She held out her arms and tugged her sister close. "I'm not mad."

"Yeah but you're disappointed, which is way worse," she sniffled against Nora's neck.

"Well, yeah, I am. Come on." She slung an arm around her sister's shoulders and pulled her to the connected shop. "Sit and I'll grab us food."

"Okay." The word came out watery as Sasha slid onto a chair at the closest high-top table.

"Let's start with why you lied to me," she said as she rounded the display counter. Her mouth watered as she pulled out the chilled triple layer chocolate cake with chocolate buttercream frosting.

"I don't know."

"That's not an answer."

"Gah, fine. Donovan is really hot and well, popular. I guess I thought if things didn't work out it would be easier if no one knew about it."

Nora slid the dessert plate and fork in front of her sister, struck by how young and vulnerable she looked at the moment. "So you figured it would hurt less if you hid your relationship?"

"I guess when you say it, it sounds dumb."

She bit back a smile. "Not dumb. It's just that you should never hide any relationship. You're one of the brightest, most beautiful girls at that school—"

Sasha snorted before stabbing her fork into her cake. "You have to say that because you're my sister."

"I don't have to say anything. And it's true, regardless. Not that your looks matter anyway. Does Donovan make you feel..." She struggled to find the right words. "Grateful he's dating you?"

"No! I mean, like, I'm glad we're together, but no. If you mean does he make me feel like he's doing me a favor or something, *no*. I'm not stupid. I'd never be with a guy like that." She snorted the last part as if it was ridiculous.

It eased some of Nora's fears. Not all of them because it was pretty clear her sister was getting physical with a boy. Something she hadn't really prepared herself for. They'd had the sex talk on multiple occasions but it had been more abstract than anything else because Sasha had never been interested in guys. Until now apparently. "Have you two had sex?" Might as well just ask the question. Nora had been older when she'd first had sex, well into college, so she'd just assumed she wouldn't have to worry about this until later.

Sasha shook her head, embarrassment clear on her face. "No. I've thought about it but I'm not ready. I don't know that I'll be ready anytime soon either."

"If you do start thinking about it, will you come to me first?" She needed to make absolutely certain that Sasha protected herself.

Sasha nodded. "I promise."

"And no more lying?

"No, I swear."

"Good. I'd like to invite your boyfriend over for dinner, get to know him better. I promise not to embarrass you—too much."

Sasha snickered. "His mom embarrasses him all the time so don't worry, there's nothing you can do worse."

"You've met his parents?"

"No. He's asked me over but I was too nervous. I've just seen her at games before. She's really loud and makes these homemade signs that all the guys hassle him about." A grin lit Sasha's face. "I think he secretly likes it though."

"You know we've been invited to Jackson's mom's house tomorrow for a Christmas Eve party. Will Donovan be there?"

"Yeah. He says he has a present for me but I didn't get him anything."

"I'm sure we can figure something out tomorrow." How hard could a teenage boy be to shop for? Apart from sex, something Nora was definitely not going to think about, they liked food, right? "Maybe you can bake him something? Or you can just get him something from Gemma's shop." The Holly Jolly Chocolatier had melt-in-your-mouth goodness on every shelf. There was no way to go wrong.

"He does eat a *lot*... So, am I, like, grounded?"

"This might be a parenting fail, but no. Tomorrow's Christmas Eve, I'm not a monster." And the truth was, Sasha was such a great kid. This whole mess aside, she'd always been so great and honest about everything.

"I think maybe you should ground me anyway," she muttered, picking at her cake now. "I've been feeling really bad. I know you were looking forward to decorating the tree and..." She trailed off, setting her fork down. "I'd feel better if you grounded me."

"You're getting a free pass for this one but only because your guilt is real. And I remember what it was like with my first boyfriend."

"Your first boyfriend was a d-bag."

Nora lifted a shoulder, not bothering to deny it as she cut off a chunk of chocolately goodness.

"Not like Jackson. What's up with you two anyway? And how did you know we were here?"

"Jackson set up video cameras and planned this whole 'sting' as he called it—"

"Ohmygodyousawus?" She shouted the question, all the words running together.

"No! I didn't even realize you were here with someone." Well, she'd suspected it considering the bra she'd found earlier. "We were watching a movie and saw you—just you—on the feed, then came over here." Thank God she hadn't seen more than that.

"Oh, good. I mean, it wasn't like we were—"

"I so don't want to hear about it. If you decide to have sex then we need to talk, but until then, I'm good." And she never wanted any details anyway. Maybe when Sasha was older and their relationship shifted they could talk about more personal things, but as of now Nora needed to keep her parental figure in place. She cleared her throat. "Listen, I think Jackson and I are going to start dating." Hopefully a lot more than just dating. There was no way to keep him at arm's length. And she didn't really want to.

"Cool. Even though he was dumb before, I like him."

"Really?"

"Yeah, he's cool. And the way he looks at you it's clear he's all about you."

Okay then. "So if he came by for Christmas breakfast, would that be okay?" She hadn't actually asked him yet, but really hoped he could.

"Totally. Can I ask Donovan too?"

"If it's okay with his parents."

The grin Sasha gave her was blinding. Suddenly Nora couldn't wait until the party tomorrow. She was going to tell Jackson that she wanted to be with him and only him. She owed it to both of them. So he'd gotten scared before? She could deal with that as long as it didn't happen again. If she was being honest, the intensity with him had scared her too. Still did, a little. She'd never imagined feeling such an intense attraction to someone. Not only that, she adored Jackson as a person. He'd always been respectful and he made her feel good about herself in a way no one ever had before. He was worth holding on to.

Plus he was sexy, protective and…he was hers.

CHAPTER SEVEN

"Stop fidgeting," Sasha muttered. "You look great." With her free hand, Nora used the old fashioned knocker on the O'Connor's front door. "I'm not fidgeting." But she was nervous. She'd decided on a bottle of wine for Jackson's mom. It seemed like a safe enough hostess gift.

"Remind me how many times you changed tonight?"

"Ha, ha. Keep pushing it and maybe I really will ground you." Nora felt a little silly being so nervous to be at Jackson's parents' place. Their long, winding driveway was filled with vehicles and the stately two-story home was lit up with an impressive display of white and multi-colored lights as well as a Santa and reindeer on their roof.

"I don't care. Donovan's grounded." She gave Nora a sly grin.

"Really? I thought he was eighteen."

"He still lives at home and apparently Jackson narced him out to his mom—"

The door opened and to Nora's surprise, Donovan opened the door. Music and laughter trickled out with him, the noise level seeming to grow with every second that ticked by. He really was a good looking kid. Tall, boyishly handsome with dark brown hair and blue eyes that seemed to run in the O'Connor family, he definitely had heartbreaker written all over him. She just hoped he didn't break her sister's heart.

He stepped forward, pulling the door shut behind him. "Miss Cassidy—"

"Call me Nora. Seriously." She was twenty-five, thank you very much.

"Yeah, sorry." He shoved his hands into the pockets of his dark slacks. His attire made her glad she'd worn a party dress. "Listen, I really wanted to apologize to you in person for sneaking around like that."

"It wasn't even his idea—" Sasha began but he cut her off with a shake of his head.

"Doesn't matter. We, *I*, shouldn't have been using your place like that. I like your sister a lot and I want to keep seeing her. I hope you don't base your opinion of me solely on this."

Nora half-smiled. He was so earnest and brave to stand there and take responsibility like this, it was hard not to. "Apology accepted. I don't know if Sasha's asked you yet, but if you'd like to join us for Christmas breakfast you're welcome to come over." She was going to ask Jackson tonight if he could make it as well and was a little nervous about it. She knew his family didn't do anything big until dinner so she hoped he'd be able to.

"Yeah, she asked and I'm in. Thanks." He looked at Sasha then, his expression softening. "You look beautiful."

"Thanks." Sasha shot Nora a look that pretty much said 'get lost' so she murmured something nonsensical and sidestepped him, opening the front door.

Nora knew Sasha wanted to give Donovan his present and she didn't need her big sister hanging around for it. And Nora didn't need to witness anything between the two of them. The foyer was festively decorated with garland and lights lining the staircase. Next to it was a white bench with a stuffed, life-sized Santa Claus holding red and silver presents in his lap. And next to that a tree that had to be at least eight feet tall was covered in fake snow and red and silver decorations.

Before she'd taken two steps, Fallon appeared out of nowhere in a slinky green dress. Her auburn hair was piled on her head in some sort of complicated twist. As usual she looked stunning, and a little flustered—which wasn't normal for her. "I'm so glad you're here." She grabbed Nora's hand and pulled her inside what turned out to be a small guest bathroom that smelled like cinnamon and vanilla. Little candles lined one of the windows, the sight of them flickering in the mirror creepy until Fallon flipped on a light.

"You okay?" Nora asked. "You seem high strung— even for you."

"Yeah, I just…might have kissed someone I definitely shouldn't have."

"Who?"

Fallon's lips pressed into a tight line. "I can't say."

"I need a drink if we're going to play this game. And I really need to find your sexy brother." Okay, maybe she didn't need a drink. She was wired and feeling practically desperate to see Jackson. They'd texted each other all day. She'd been crazy busy but had made the time for him. The anticipation of seeing him had her feeling almost buzzed.

Fallon's mouth dropped open for a fraction of a second. "Are you two finally..." She made an obscene thrusting motion with her hips.

Feeling her cheeks heat up, Nora nodded. "You are such a guy, I swear. And yeah, I think so. I just need to talk to him." And kiss him because it was all she'd been thinking about today. Straddling him on her couch last night, then having to stop, had been the last straw. She needed Jackson's mouth on hers as soon as possible, and his body on top of hers as soon as possible after that.

"Well come on. Get that coat off and give me that bottle of wine."

"That's for your mom and she better get it," Nora said, laughing.

"No promises. Now come on, give me the coat." Fallon held out a hand as Nora slid her black coat off to reveal a red dress that would have been way too expensive if she hadn't gotten it on sale at eighty percent off.

Formfitting, it had a lace overlay and fit all her curves to perfection. It was like the thing had been made for her. With her four-inch heels and their thin straps wrapping around her ankles, she knew she looked good. It gave her the confidence she needed to put herself out there completely for Jackson.

Fallon let out a low whistle. "My brother's totally a goner. If you guys get married I better be one of your bridesmaids—and the dress better not suck."

Nora probably should have been taken back by that statement but the truth was, she could see a future with Jackson. And she wanted it more than she'd wanted anything. "Deal. And I want to know who you kissed."

Fallon mimed zipping her lips and throwing away the key.

"I'll find you later after you've had a few glasses of champagne and we'll see how quiet you are then," she said as she opened the door.

"Ha, ha. I'm going to put your coat in the front closet, okay? I saw Jackson in the living room earlier." She pointed to the nearest open entryway, also decorated with garland and lights. Man, the O'Connors didn't mess around with Christmas.

"Yeah. Oh, wait." She reached into the pocket and pulled out the sprig of fake mistletoe she'd brought with her. If she lost her nerve she just planned to hold this over his head.

Fallon just laughed and headed for the foyer. Now Nora was on a mission.

"You've got to be kidding me," she muttered the second she stepped into the packed room. Nolan and Maguire, Jackson's two brothers, were in a lively debate about something to do with beer, the elderly Baker sisters were definitely on the way from tipsy to having to be carried out and Angelia had her manicured nails brushing up against Jackson's forearm as they stood next to the fireplace.

For the briefest moment, stupid insecurities flared wild and hot inside Nora...

Until she read Jackson's body language.

His jaw was clenched and his shoulders were stiff as he took a small step back from the petite blonde. It was almost imperceptible but she could practically see him making his getaway.

Well, she could help with that. Someone called her name but she ignored them and made her way across the plush, festive room, smiling at the Baker sisters, who were perched on the edge of a couch, talking animatedly to each other.

Jackson looked up and saw her when she was about three feet from him and the mixture of relief and hunger in his eyes was almost enough to make her stop in her tracks. Yeah, she had nothing to worry about. Never with Jackson.

She didn't even bother to look at Angelia, just held up the mistletoe and grinned at Jackson.

He murmured something that sounded a lot like "hell yeah" before he crushed his mouth to hers. She felt the claiming—and that's exactly what it was—all the way to her toes. His tongue flicked against hers with a heated urgency, probably a little too long in a setting like this before he pulled back, his breathing erratic.

"You're mine," he murmured, his expression hard, as if he was daring her to argue.

"I know."

He blinked those beautiful blue eyes as if he'd been expecting an argument or something. "Officially."

"I know," she murmured, sliding her hands around his waist. She was vaguely aware of the people, music and pretty lights, but all she could focus on was Jackson. She couldn't wait to be alone with him later.

He narrowed his eyes. "As in you're my girlfriend now."

A laugh bubbled up inside her and it felt so damn good. "Do you think I need convincing? I'm agreeing with you."

"Good." His expression was as fierce and possessive as his grip around her. "I don't even care if my mom wins the bet—"

"Bet?"

He snorted. "Apparently there was a bet—that I just found out about—that started at Silver Bells on when we'd make things official. The pot's over six hundred bucks, I think. Plus some other stuff."

"We should have gotten in on that action!"

He blinked once before that wicked grin that had completely stolen her heart—and breath—widened. "God, I love you."

Before she could respond his mouth was on hers again, teasing and delicious, until one of his brothers told them to get a room.

"That's not a bad idea," she murmured, pulling back from him. Angelia was thankfully long gone now and Nora didn't care where she was. "But first, champagne."

"Sounds good to me." He slid his arm around her shoulders in that familiar, possessive way and it felt like the most natural action in the world.

Being with Jackson felt like coming home.

CHAPTER EIGHT

Nora rolled over in bed at the incessant ringing. What the heck? It took her a moment to realize it was her phone. She grabbed it from her nightstand after two tries and barely made out Jackson's name and picture on the screen. Gah, the screen was way too bright in her dark room. She held her arm over her eyes.

"Hello? What's wrong?" Because there was no reason he was calling for anything other than an emergency at four in the morning.

"I'm downstairs. Let me in." His deep voice had the usual effect even if she was half asleep.

"What?"

"I'm freezing out here. Come on, I've got a present for you."

"Is that like a euphemism?"

His laughter warmed her straight to her toes. "No. Come on, it's cold."

"Hold on," she mock grumbled.

Forcing herself out of bed, she snagged her robe from the back of her bathroom door and cinched it around her waist—then quickly brushed her teeth for good measure. If he was here, there was a good chance kissing would be involved. They'd spent most of the party last night together, then a little after midnight he'd had to head back to his place to get the rocking chair he'd made for his dad. She'd taken Sasha home and had finished wrapping up the last few presents for her sister. Nora knew she'd gone a little overboard this year for Sasha but she didn't care. Next year she'd be eighteen and likely off to college so Nora wanted to spoil her just a little more. Besides, it made up for all the years of their mom doing nothing.

Downstairs she turned off the alarm. Jackson barreled inside on a gust of icy wind with a cloth bag in his hand. As soon as he'd shut and locked the door his mouth was on hers, his cold, gloved hands cupping her cheeks.

Even that couldn't chill her, not with his tongue invading her mouth, teasing and taking. She clutched on to his shoulders to steady herself until he pulled back. Though she still didn't let go.

"I missed you," he murmured, his eyes raking over her face as if he could devour her.

She'd missed him too. "It's only been a couple hours."

He winced slightly. "Sorry for waking you up."

"No you're not. And I'm not either." She slid her arms around him, the chill of his body against hers and just his presence making her nipples tighten. She'd wanted some private time with him earlier, but between the party, and then getting Sasha home it just hadn't been in the cards.

The grin slid right into place, making her heart melt. "I'm really not," he murmured. "You want your present?"

If it involved him naked in her bed, yes.

She nodded and after he tugged his boots off, she pulled him into the living room. She'd left the Christmas tree lights on, but turned on one of the lamps. She was finally going to get to experience all of Jackson—and she didn't plan to let him go. "Did you get the rocking chair to your parents' house?"

"Yeah, my mom helped me sneak it into the garage."

"I'm sure your dad will love it."

"I hope so." Without warning, he tugged her into his lap as he sat on the couch. The cloth bag he'd brought was next to him. "I like being able to touch and kiss you any time I want."

"Me too." She brushed her lips over his, savoring his taste. She liked that he could touch her and kiss her anytime too. No more denying her feelings. If things didn't work out between them it would shred her up, but she couldn't go into this relationship expecting the worst to happen. That was a complete recipe for disaster and the truth was, she saw something real with Jackson.

He was the first to pull back, much to her surprise. "I didn't have time to wrap this one," he said as he reached into the bag, "And I probably should have just waited until nine to bring this but I needed to see you." The raw hunger in his voice mirrored her own feelings.

"I'm glad you didn't wait." She let out a little gasp as he placed the hand-carved jewelry box in her hands. "This is beautiful. What kind of wood is this?" She ran her fingers over the intricate ivy and vine carvings along the top.

"Walnut."

There were so many details it was unbelievable. The 'N' in the middle with butterflies somehow intricately carved as if they were flying through the letter made her smile. It was even more special because he'd made this with his own hands. "Thank you feels inadequate. This is amazing," she said, looking at him now. "Thank you for something so thoughtful and beautiful."

His cheeks flushed slightly and he gave a half-shrug. She'd noticed he didn't take praise well. "Open it."

It opened up to two compartments, both lined with a soft, pale blue velvet.

"If you slide this panel out..." He moved the front lower panel to the left, and another panel inside slid open to reveal a small secret compartment. "You should put expensive stuff in a safe anyway, but I thought you'd like this."

"You're amazing, Jackson." Cupping his cheeks, she intended to just brush her lips over his and pull back so she could give him his present, but the moment they made contact she swore she could feel something shift inside him.

He let out a sort of growling sound and crushed his mouth to hers. All her nerve endings flared to life as his tongue teased against her.

She was vaguely aware of him moving the jewelry box off her lap before he suddenly stood, scooping her up in his arms. She let out a soft gasp, realizing what he intended—and what she wanted. "My sister's here."

"She's asleep upstairs, right?"

MERRY CHRISTMAS, BABY | 87

Nora nodded. And her sister was a heavy sleeper too. She wouldn't be up for at least a few more hours. "I've got a present for you too though."

"Give me another present first," he murmured, a question in his eyes. Did she want this? That was an easy answer. "Upstairs, now." The words were barely out before he'd moved into action. "Second door on the right." Luckily the bedrooms were across the hall, not next door to each other.

His mouth was on hers again by the time they reached it. She didn't have time to think or care that her room was a little messy before she heard the snick then lock of her bedroom door.

Jackson moved with an incredible efficiency, carrying her as if she weighed nothing, until he had her splayed out on the bed. "Tell me if you want to stop." His voice was surprisingly unsteady as he stood back.

Her heart was pounding. She was glad to know she wasn't the only one so affected. "No way." Moonlight and streetlights streamed in from her two windows to give them more than enough illumination. "Now strip." Because he'd already seen her naked once and she desperately wanted to see all of him.

As he started stripping off his jacket, then his long-sleeved sweater, she sat up and slid out of her robe—but pretty much froze when he tugged the sweater completely over his head. Washboard abs that should be illegal tightened under her scrutiny. He was like a work of art, all those stark lines and striations absolute perfection.

She wasn't sure how long she stared until he cupped her cheek, then slid his fingers back into her hair. The way he swept his gaze over her face was so full of lust and hunger, her breath caught in her throat. He tugged her hair slightly as he tilted her head to his. The tiny bite made her suck in a breath. His expression was intense as he looked at her, his blue eyes seemingly darker in the dimness of her room. It was so quiet right now, the only sounds permeating the room their harsh breathing. The intimacy of it made her feel as if they were the only two people in the world.

"I wasn't kidding what I said earlier. I love you, Nora."

She'd been wondering if it had been just one of those slips at his parents' place earlier. To hear him say the words now with a look of such love on his face, made her throat tighten with emotion.

"I love you too." Saying the words out loud was a little terrifying. Meeting and falling for someone like Jackson had never been in her plans. Heck, she'd never imagined there was someone as wonderful as him out there.

His mouth was on hers again, demanding and taking everything she had to give. She fell back against the sheets as he climbed on top of her, his body covering her with all that warmth.

She slid her fingers down his chest and abs, tracing her fingers along the ridges of his abdomen, moving lower and lower until he grasped her by the wrists. Before she could ask why he was stopping her, he held her hands above her head, his mouth hovering right over hers.

On instinct she arched into him, wanting more skin to skin contact.

"No touching me until you've come against my mouth." His words were a soft order she felt all the way to her toes.

If it had been possible to physically melt, she would have done so on the spot. That was probably the hottest thing anyone had ever said to her. Combined with the expression on his face that said he meant every word, and yeah, she was a goner.

Moving with that sexy predatory grace, he released her wrists and shifted down the bed. When he tugged her pajama pants and panties off in a quick move, she couldn't stop the thrill of hunger that shot through her.

"I've fantasized about this," she murmured.

He froze, his big palms stilling on her inner knees as he crouched between her legs. But for only an instant. "My mouth on you?"

She nodded and shimmied out of her top, completely baring herself to him. When their gazes connected she felt insanely powerful at the lust practically vibrating off him. All that hunger was for her and her alone. He'd seen her before when she'd been on his lap straddling him after that first date. He'd licked and teased her nipples with his mouth and made her come with his oh-so-talented fingers.

But then he'd put the brakes on, not wanting to rush. Now to be stretched out for him, completely bare like this, was exhilarating. She hadn't been naked in front of a man in years other than him, and she didn't feel an ounce of anxiety with Jackson. Because he would never hurt her. She could see that promise in his eyes.

"I've also thought about my mouth on *you*. A lot," she continued, her voice dropping a few octaves.

His fingers tightened around her knees. Cool air rushed over her exposed body. She loved the way he stilled, loved seeing that she affected him as much as he did her. Her nipples hardened even more and heat flooded between her legs as she watched him. He was still crouched between her legs but those words seemed to light him on fire.

Groaning, he took her by surprise when he buried his face between her legs with no warning. She arched into him, her hips rolling instinctively. "Jackson," she rasped out his name as he tongued her clit with enough pressure to drive her crazy.

He moaned against her, the vibration increasing her sensitivity to his teasing.

She slid her fingers through his inky black hair, holding onto the dark strands as he flicked his tongue up the length of her folds. She was already so wet for him she knew it wouldn't take long for her to come. But she felt almost empty inside, desperate with the need for him to fill her.

He'd yet to take off his pants so she still hadn't gotten a look at him—and she had definitely fantasized. Just the thought of seeing him completely exposed to her as well, of getting to stroke him with her hand, then mouth—

"You're so wet," he murmured as he slipped a finger inside her.

"Because of you." He groaned again at that. She couldn't respond when he slid another thick digit inside her. Her inner walls tightened around him as he pushed deep, his tongue working magic against her clit. The sensitive bundle of nerves ached and throbbed, her release just out of reach.

When he began moving his fingers inside her faster, she pushed right over that edge. "Jackson." His name came out like a prayer as her body bowed tight under the onslaught of that first cresting wave.

Streams of pleasure spiraled out to all her nerve endings as he curved his fingers at just the right angle, dragging them against her inner wall as he wreaked havoc on her clit. Her climax punched through her, completely taking over until the only thing she was aware of was Jackson's face between her legs and his wicked, wicked tongue.

She wasn't sure if she cried out too loudly or what she said, she was too lost in her pleasure. By the time she collapsed back against the sheet, panting and sated, she looked down to find him watching her intently.

Wordlessly he withdrew his fingers from her and she immediately felt the loss. The empty ache between her legs was even worse now. She needed to feel him inside her like she needed her next breath. When he slid his wet fingers between his lips she sucked in a sharp breath.

If what he'd said earlier was the hottest thing she'd heard, then this was the hottest thing she'd ever *seen*.

"Love your taste." He closed his eyes for a long moment, seemed to savor her.

Oh yeah, she'd completely fallen for Jackson O'Connor, no doubt about it. Now it was her turn. Her body buzzing with the aftereffects of her orgasm, she sat up and reached for the button of his jeans, but he moved fast, sliding off the bed.

"Not coming in your hands." His jaw was tight, his expression warrior-fierce as he shucked his jeans.

When his erection was freed, her eyes widened. Long and thick, he was definitely big all over. She wanted to trace every inch of it with her tongue. Even the thought of that had her nipples tightening even more.

"You on the pill?" he rasped out as he grabbed a condom from his discarded pants.

"Yeah, for years." For health reasons, none of which she wanted to talk about right now. She just wanted to feel him inside her.

At her words, his hands stilled. "I'm clean. I was tested over six months ago and I haven't been with anyone since then."

"Me too." And it had been a lot longer than six months. "We don't need to use the condom," she said, answering his unspoken question.

"You sure?"

"If you are."

He dropped it like it was on fire. "I can't go slow this time."

"Good." She didn't want that, not now, not when she felt like a giant mass of trembling energy.

Then he was on her, his mouth covering hers as he reached between their bodies. Despite the fact that he'd just felt her climax against him, he cupped her mound and tested her slickness—and shuddered. She loved the feel of his callused hands on the most sensitive part of her.

She spread her legs wider for him, wrapping them around his waist. The feel of his bare chest against hers was the most erotic sensation. She wanted to rub up against him like a cat in heat. She knew she should be sated, but as he shifted slightly, nudging his thick erection between her folds, she wanted more.

"Nora," he groaned out her name as he looked down at her, his gaze full of too many emotions for her to filter. His muscular arms caged her in on either side.

She lifted her hips, not wanting to wait a second longer, impaling herself on him.

He hissed in a breath as he filled her. All his features seemed sharper as he kept his eyes pinned on hers. To have him watching her so intently felt incredibly intimate. Even if she wanted to, she couldn't look away. Then he started thrusting inside her, slowly at first until his movements were unsteady and wild.

She met him stroke for stroke, savoring the way he completely filled her with each thrust. His jaw clenched tight and though she'd never seen him come before, she guessed he was close. She ran her fingers up his abdomen, over his chest then his strong arms. It was as if the man had been carved from stone, everything about him utter perfection. The scars and nicks covering his body only added to his ridiculous sex appeal.

And he was all hers.

That knowledge pushed her over the edge again. She simply let go of any semblance of control and let the orgasm rip through her. Just like that, he came too, with a shout that sounded a lot like triumph as he buried his face against her neck.

She wrapped her arms around him, clutched him to her as he emptied himself inside her. She wasn't sure how long it took before they both came back to themselves, but eventually her breathing evened out. And Jackson hadn't made any attempt to move off her.

He just nuzzled her neck as he stroked those big hands over her breasts and hips. It was as if he couldn't get enough of touching her. And it didn't seem to matter that he was half-hard in her now, he just wanted to touch her. Definitely fine with her. She couldn't wait to explore more of him. She wanted everything from him, to move in with him, maybe...even more one day.

"Merry Christmas, baby," he murmured, sounding surprisingly drowsy.

She grinned, stroking her fingers down his muscular back. "Best Christmas present ever." And she was never letting him go.

EPILOGUE

Jackson wiped his palms on his jeans as he sat at one of the high-top tables waiting for Nora to lock up her shop. Tonight was it. He was proposing because there was no way he could go another day without claiming her forever for everyone to see. Dating wasn't enough for him. He wanted everything and he wanted his ring on her finger so the entire world knew she was his.

Caveman attitude? Yep. He didn't care.

He'd gone on countless missions where he'd been sure he would die and he'd never felt an ounce of the fear he experienced now. What if she said no? Things between them were incredible, and the sex... He couldn't think about that now. Otherwise he'd start kissing her the moment she joined him and they'd end up naked in her storeroom.

Again.

The past two months had been the best of his life and he couldn't imagine not having Nora in his life forever. He wanted to move in with her but she'd told him not until Sasha was out of the house. Which he respected. He liked that she was setting a good example for her sister, but if they were married, they didn't have to wait. And he wasn't waiting any longer.

"You okay?" Nora asked, her expression worried as she walked up to him, her boots clicking softly on the tile of the café floor as she reached him. In just a couple months it would be spring and she'd be wearing those sexy dresses again. He couldn't wait.

Clearing his throat, he nodded. "Yeah, just want to make those reservations." He'd booked a table for them at her favorite place and planned to propose afterward once they had privacy. It was almost Valentine's Day so she didn't seem suspicious about the reservations. He was going to suggest they take a walk down Main Street since it was a perfect moonlit night and it wasn't far from her favorite park. Tonight needed to be perfect.

She let out a light laugh. "We've got plenty of time." She gave him a quick kiss on the lips before moving through the throng of high-top tables. "You want some tea or something? I've just got to run the end of the night reports. It won't take long."

"I'm okay but I'll make you something." He slid off the stool and trailed after her, rounding the counter as she did.

Nora gave him another curious look as he practically ran into her. Turning, she placed her hands on her hips. "All right, what's going on?"

He kept his expression blank. "Nothing."

"Are you breaking up with me?"

"No!"

She snickered and he realized she hadn't been serious. "I didn't actually think that, but jeez, what's going on?"

Gently, she ran her hands down his upper arms and forearms. "You're all tight... Is something wrong at work? Or with your family?" She sounded horrified at the last question.

"No, nothing like that." He tried to force himself to relax but he simply couldn't. God, he'd never felt like this in his life, as if he could crawl out of his own skin from raw fear that she would say no.

Jackson hadn't even realized he was moving until he'd pulled the small jewelry box from his jacket pocket and was on one knee before her. But hell, he couldn't wait another second. The desire to see his ring on her finger, to officially start their life together, was overwhelming to the point he could barely think straight.

She blinked down at him, her green eyes filled with confusion until he held open the box.

With trembling fingers, he flipped it open. "Marry me?"

When tears filled her eyes, panic set in, but only for a moment. Her smile was blinding as she nodded. "Yes!" She practically tackled him as she threw her arms around his neck.

They would have both tumbled to the floor if he hadn't steadied them. Relief like he'd never known flowed through him, hot and fierce. He had the ring out and on her left hand ring finger as she wiped tears from her eyes with her other hand.

"It's beautiful," she said, not even looking at it as she cupped his cheeks. "I love you so much, Jackson."

"I wanted to do it right, take you to dinner and—"

She shook her head. "This is right, it's perfect."

"You're perfect." They argued like any other couple but she was everything he'd been looking for when he hadn't even known he was looking.

Laughing, she shook her head. "I don't know what I did to deserve you."

"Right back at you." He was never letting her go. "I love you, Nora. And I don't want to wait to get married, I want to do it this year." Living apart the past two months had been sheer torture. He'd stayed over at her place, sure, but it wasn't the same thing as waking up to her beautiful face every morning.

"It's only February, that leaves a lot of months to plan—"

He shook his head. "A spring wedding."

Her eyes widened so he crushed his mouth to hers, taking away any argument she might have had. He wanted to go to bed with her every night and wake up with her every morning. When she tightened her grip around him and groaned into his mouth, he figured they were probably going to be late for their reservation after all.

He didn't mind one bit. Not when the woman he loved had just agreed to become his wife.

Thank you for reading Merry Christmas, Baby. If you don't want to miss any future releases, please feel free to join my newsletter. I only send out a newsletter for new releases or sales news. Find the signup link on my website: http://www.katiereus.com

MIAMI, MISTLETOE & MURDER EXCERPT
Red Stone Security Series
Copyright © 2012 Katie Reus

Travis Sanchez rubbed a hand over his head as he stepped into the elevator at the Red Stone Security building. His mohawk was gone and he wore his hair in a buzz cut these days. It was probably his military background, but he always came back to this cut out of habit.

The walk to Harrison's office was too short. He wasn't sure why his boss had called him in after the last security detail, but a small burst of panic had detonated in his gut. He loved this job, but there had been some issues with the CEO he'd recently been guarding not following Travis's orders. The asshole had almost gotten himself killed and now Travis wondered if his head was on the chopping block because of it.

The assistant's desk in the outer office was empty, so he strode through to Lizzy Caldwell's office. Lizzy was Harrison's sister-in-law and wicked scary on a computer. Sitting behind her desk, the dark-haired woman smiled and held up a finger when she saw him. She wasn't holding a phone to her ear, but he could see the earpiece in. She nodded and made monosyllabic answers to whoever was on the other end before hanging up.

"Finally," she muttered as she stood and hurried around the desk. Taking him by surprise, she gave him a tight hug. "It's been too long, Travis. I like your new haircut."

He awkwardly patted her back. She was affectionate and had hugged him a few times in the past, but now he wondered if maybe he really was getting fired. "Thanks." After thirty-six hours of no sleep, he was tired, grungy and... "Holy shit, are you pregnant?" The question popped out before he could stop himself. His mom had taught him to *never* ask a woman that unless he was absolutely sure and even then, he should keep his fat mouth shut. But he'd felt a bump as she hugged him. "I mean..."

Laughing, she stepped back and gently patted his arm. "Yes, about four and a half months now. Harrison's expecting you so just go on in. I want to hear all about your last job later though." Her smile was reassuring so maybe he wasn't getting fired. Maybe he'd just get yelled at.

As he stepped inside, his eyes widened. The office was all windows—bullet resistant glass for sure because Red Stone Security didn't mess around—and had a great view of downtown Miami, but that wasn't what he was staring at. There was a golf set and two broken clubs on the west side of the expansive room. He'd rarely seen Harrison lose his temper, but he wondered if he'd broken them. The man had a slow burn kind of thing he did when he was angry and got really quiet before raining hell down. It was damn intimidating.

"Don't ask," Harrison muttered before motioning for Travis to sit.

Wordlessly, he did as his boss asked.

"Glad you're back in Miami in one piece. Sorry you had to deal with that asshole, Cranston." Harrison typed away on his computer as he spoke, but Travis had no doubt the man's attention was focused on him. His boss could multi-task like no one he'd ever seen.

Travis's eyebrows rose, but he didn't respond because he wasn't sure if he was supposed to. Barry Cranston had been one of the biggest assholes he'd ever been assigned to. The dick had actually requested that Travis find him a prostitute. As if that was even remotely part of his job. But, he'd guarded the man and almost taken a bullet for him so no one could say he hadn't done his damn job.

Harrison finally looked at him, his dark eyes unreadable. "Starting today, you're on paid vacation for a week."

Travis blinked. "What?"

"You deserve a fucking break and I know you'll never take one so the next seven days are yours to do whatever you want. Go fishing or...whatever. You'll be paid and it won't count against your accrued vacation days."

"I'm not getting fired?" What was wrong with him? He couldn't seem to rein in his big mouth today. Travis scrubbed a hand over his face. Man he really needed to sleep.

Harrison's head tilted slightly to the side. "Why...because of Cranston? Fuck no. We're never working with that asshole again. If we gave out medals, I'd give you one for putting up with his bullshit."

"Oh. Then why the vacation? I don't need one." The last job had been stressful, but not much more than normal. Travis would be the first to admit if he was getting close to burnout and he was nowhere near that. Besides,

106 | KATIE REUS

it was nearing Christmas and he'd rather keep busy. His sister was living up north and he didn't have any other living family. The holidays weren't his favorite time of year anymore. Not since his mom passed away. She'd made everything perfect around Christmas but... He mentally shook himself.

Harrison grunted and stood. "You're taking one and that's that."

By the look on his boss's face, Travis knew he wasn't getting more of an answer. Okay, then. If Harrison said he was taking time off, he had no choice. Following suit, he stood. "Thanks, boss. If something comes up, call me but if not I'll check in next Friday."

Half smiling, Harrison rounded the desk and gave him a shoulder squeeze as they walked to the door. "Nothing will come up. Enjoy your time off."

After talking to Lizzy for a few minutes, Travis made his way back to the elevators and out of the expansive multi-story building into the chilly December air. Even though he was in the business district, the city was definitely in the holiday spirit. There were a few giant wreaths completely made of lights on some of the buildings off Brickell Avenue. Poles were lined with twinkly lights depicting Christmas trees, candles and of course the palm trees were strung up with lights. He wished he could get more into the spirit, but it was a struggle.

Instead of parking in the employee garage, he'd parked his truck a couple blocks over on Flagler so he'd have an excuse to stop at the coffee shop he'd been frequenting for the past year. Whenever he was in town, he found himself heading over there before and after work. Pathetic, but he didn't care. Noel, the tall, lithe owner with a mass of dark curly hair and pale grayish eyes, had been the subject of his fantasies for the better part of the year. She was always friendly to him whenever he was in her shop and she sometimes sat and talked with him—something he'd noticed she didn't do with anyone else—but he couldn't figure out if she was just being polite.

It was nearing six, which meant she'd be closing soon so he picked up his pace. He passed a few people on the street, all of them bundled up wearing hats and coats, an odd sight in normally sweltering Miami. As he neared her shop, he slowed down and forced himself to get his shit together. For all he knew, she wasn't even working. Before he'd reached the door, Noel of all people, walked out. Carrying an oversized purse and looking at her cell phone, she didn't even glance up. He tried to move out of the way but she slammed into him.

Her purse slid off her shoulder as her head snapped back. Wide eyes met his and her mouth formed a small 'O' as he steadied her. He gently held her upper arms as she stared at him for a long moment. She was slender, but not exactly fragile. There was a subtle strength he'd picked up on the first time they'd met.

"Travis." She practically breathed his name. It was like a seductive caress, but then she shook her head and that's when he realized her pale eyes were bright with unshed tears.

He automatically tensed, hating to see any woman cry, but especially her. "What's wrong?"

Glancing away from him, she shook her head and bent to pick up her purse.

Kneeling with her, he started gathering some of the things that had fallen out and nearly choked when his fingers wrapped around a box of condoms with a red bow wrapped around it.

"Oh my...that's not...well, it is mine. One of my friends gave it to me as a gag gift for my birthday." She snatched it out of his hand and shoved it into the mammoth black bag she called a purse.

Travis struggled to talk, as he always did around her. Thinking about her and condoms in the same sentence was threatening to short-circuit his brain. He hated his reaction because it made him feel like a randy teenager with a crush. Which is basically what he had on her. A giant crush. Her tan cheeks were a bright crimson as she met his gaze again. At least he didn't see tears in her eyes anymore. He couldn't handle the thought of her upset.

"You leaving? I thought I might catch you before you got off work." He was pretty sure his sleep-deprived brain had taken over but he wouldn't complain. He needed to ask her out and if she rejected him, he'd get over it and find another place to get coffee.

Her face brightened for a moment, her cheeks flushing even darker. "Really?" Before he could answer she sharply shook her head. "Uh, I've got to go. I don't have time to talk right now, Travis. But I'll see you later." Now the stress was back, full force. It was so potent, it was practically surging off her in visible waves.

As she started to hurry down the sidewalk to the end of her building where she usually parked, he fell in step with her. "What's going on, Noel?" He'd never seen her like this before. Normally she had a bright smile for everyone.

She gave him a guarded look and he could practically see the wheels turning in her head. He'd taken out his ear and eyebrow piercings for his last job but he still had visible tattoos and, for some reason, he felt as if she was sizing him up. Finally she sighed as they rounded the corner of the building. "I mentor as a Big Sister and Juanita, that's my mentee's name, called me a few minutes ago and she's really worried. Her mother's ex-boyfriend has been hanging around lately and she swears he's never been abusive to her, but he's been giving her the creeps. He only stops by when her mother is working and she said she thought she saw him drive by more than once."

Adrenaline punched through him. Noel was tall and lean with a runner's body so she wasn't some fragile thing, but still... "You're going over there by yourself?"

She shot him an annoyed glance. "Yeah."

"Do you know anything about this guy? If he has a record, or possible weapons or—"

"I don't know anything other than Juanita is scared. I tried calling the cops but they said they couldn't do anything other than send a patrol car down the street."

He admired her protective response but he wasn't letting her walk into a situation like this alone. "I'm going with you," he said as they reached her green, four-door hybrid car.

"Excuse me?" She looked up at him now, her keys dangling from her left hand.

Bending down, he lifted his pants pocket where he had a weapon holstered. "I have a permit and you already know who I work for. What harm can it do to have me along? If the guy is there, chances are he'll be more apt to walk away if I'm with you." People tended not to fuck with him because of his outward appearance. And if they did anyway, they learned fast that he fought dirty and took down his enemies any way he could. When she bit her bottom lip but didn't respond, he continued. "Think about what's best for Juanita."

At those words, he could see the decision made in her eyes. Even though she still looked slightly unsure, she nodded. "Get in."

* * *

Noel gripped her steering wheel tight, using it to ground herself. When she'd heard Juanita's panicked tone, fear had taken over. She'd met that piece of crap, Dwight Gomez, before Juanita's mother had broken up with him and she didn't like the way he looked at the young girl. She was only fourteen.

"So, condoms, huh?" Travis, the man she'd been lusting after for six months, asked.

Since they were at a stoplight, she glanced at him in surprise. The man was so hard to read sometimes. He rarely smiled, but his expression was never harsh or anything. He was just…reserved. Noel never had a problem talking to people, but she was occasionally tongue-tied around Travis. That was because she was constantly wondering what he would look like naked. She'd seen flashes of tattoos—some around the neckline of his shirt and a few on his arms—and she really wanted to see how much of his body was covered in them. Before meeting him she'd never thought having ink on your body was sexy but Travis…the man was delicious. Since he didn't seem like the kind of man to ever purposefully embarrass someone, she had a pretty good idea what he was doing. "Are you trying to distract me?"

He shrugged those impossibly broad shoulders she'd love to smooth her hands over. "Maybe."

Feeling her damn cheeks heat up under that intense gaze, she turned back to the road. When the light turned green, she sighed. "One of my employees—also a dear friend—thinks I need to get laid and thought it would be a funny birthday present. So she got me condoms and stuff."

"Happy birthday. What do you mean by stuff?" There was a note of amusement and real curiosity in that last word.

She cleared her throat. Um, yeah, she was definitely not telling him that her friend had also gotten her flavored lube, a pink whip, a purple rubber paddle and vibrating nipple suckers. Until today she hadn't even known nipple suckers existed. "We are not having this conversation. So, why were you hoping to catch me before I got off work?" *Please let it be because you wanted to ask me out.* She'd thought about asking him out herself, but the man was just so hard to read. Whenever she worked up the courage, he'd disappear for weeks at a time. She knew it was for his job, but then by the time he would start regularly visiting her shop again, her courage would go back into hibernation. He just had that intimidating effect on her.

He shifted against the passenger seat, his long legs looking cramped even though he'd pushed the seat all the way back. She was five feet ten so she guessed him to be six feet three. Give or take. "I wanted to see if you had plans tomorrow night. If not, I'd like to take you out to dinner and maybe we can walk around Bayside Marketplace afterward." He said the words in a rush, as if he'd been practicing.

Which made her feel a lot better. Despite the way her day was going and the worry building inside her over

Juanita, elation burst inside her. Still, she needed to understand what he was asking. "Would this be as friends or a date?"

He paused a long moment. "I was hoping for a date." And there it was. Finally. Fighting the giant grin on her face, she nodded. "Okay."

The tension in the car seemed to crackle for a moment until her ringing cell cut through the air. When she saw Juanita's number, panic surged through her again. Noel had told Juanita to turn off the lights in the house and pretend she wasn't home. She just hoped the girl had listened. "Hey." She answered on the first ring, putting the girl on speaker so she'd have her hands free.

"My mom got home from work early and she and Dwight are in the driveway arguing. I don't know what to do." Fear and tears laced her voice.

"Where are you right now?"

"I did what you said, but then I heard shouting. He's holding onto her arm and she's yelling at him. I don't know what to do." Juanita let out a sob.

"Do you have a backyard?" Travis asked, before Noel could speak.

There was a moment of silence so Noel said, "Honey, this is Travis. He's a friend and he's coming with me to help."

"Okay. And yeah, we have a backyard."

"Is it possible for you to make it to your backyard without being seen?" Travis asked.

Juanita sniffled. "Yeah."

"Good. Forget what's going on in the driveway. Get the hell out of your house. Sneak out back, climb a fence, whatever it takes. Just stay hidden and call the cops. They'll listen to you when you tell them what's happening." There was no room for argument in Travis's voice.

Noel was so grateful for his presence. She'd been scared of having to face that jerk alone and now she was just worried for Juanita and her mom. "Juanita, listen to what he says. I know you want to help your mom, but there's nothing you can do now. Get out of that house. We'll be there in two minutes."

"Okay," she whispered. "Stay on the line with me."

"We're not going anywhere, honey." Out of the corner of her eye, Noel watched as Travis pulled out his cell phone. He began texting furiously then asked for Juanita's address. Noel gave it to him while listening to Juanita moving through her house. She heard the squeak of a door opening. She could faintly hear shouting in the background.

"I can hear them," Juanita whispered.

"I can too. Just do what I say. Your mom will want you to be safe more than anything." The young girl's mother, Alisa, worked two jobs to provide for Juanita. She was caring, hardworking and though she'd never said it, Noel was pretty certain the reason she'd ended things with Dwight was because of the way he'd been eyeing her daughter. Noel knew from past girls she'd mentored that not all moms were that caring. Sad, but true.

"Okay, I'm climbing the fence to my neighbor's yard. I've got to put the phone down for a sec, don't hang up!"

"I won't, I promise." They'd be there in less than thirty seconds. "We're close, Travis."

There was a rustling sound then she was back on the line. "Okay, I'm hiding behind the shed in my neighbor's backyard. He won't be home for another two hours."

"Good, stay there. And don't worry about contacting the police. I've taken care of it," Travis said.

Noel wondered who he'd texted, but figured it must be someone he worked with. She didn't know all the specifics of who exactly ran Red Stone Security but she'd heard rumors and she knew for a fact that a lot of former military people—Travis being one—and law enforcement worked for them to protect really wealthy people. She guessed Travis must have connections or something.

Before Noel could say anything she heard a loud boom in the background. Next to her Travis tensed, his entire body going on alert.

"Juanita, do not get out of your hiding place," Travis ordered.

"But, what was that? Did you guys hear—"

"Stay where you are!" Noel shouted as realization dawned. That had been a gunshot. Her heart beat an erratic tattoo as they turned down Juanita's street. It was a nice neighborhood with neatly kept lawns. Lower middle class with all working families and a lot of kids.

"Park here and stay on the phone with her. Whatever happens, don't you dare follow me." Travis motioned to a yellow one-story ranch style house with red trim on the shutters. The two palm trees in the yard were strung up with Christmas lights.

Noel nodded, stark fear latching onto her chest. "What are you going to do?" she asked even though she was pretty sure she knew the answer. There was a determined glint in his dark eyes she'd never seen before.

He didn't respond, just slid from her car like a ghost. She watched as he crept down the sidewalk toward Juanita's house, four homes down. Taking her by surprise, he hurried into a neighbor's yard then disappeared from sight. In the distance she could hear sirens and just prayed they were coming for them. If Alisa had been injured...Noel shuddered, unwilling to think that. She said a silent prayer that everyone would be fine.

* * *

Even with his lack of sleep, the adrenaline that pumped through Travis's system had completely revived him. That had definitely been a gunshot and he hoped he got to Juanita's mother in time. To think that Noel had planned to come over here on her own—he shoved that thought away.

Now was the time to focus on diffusing whatever was going on. He'd texted Grant Caldwell, who was Harrison's brother and a former detective with the Miami PD.

The newest Red Stone employee had gotten back to him immediately telling him that help was on the way.

But Juanita's mom might not have time. Dusk had just fallen so it was dark enough for him to blend into the shadows. Something he was damn good at. After eight years in Force Recon, most of those spent in violent warzones, he knew how to be invisible.

Weapon in hand, he jumped fences and ran until he reached the address Noel had given him. Creeping along the neighbor's house, he moved until he had a perfect view of Juanita's home. There were two cars in the driveway along with a woman's purse. The belongings had been strewn in the yard and on the driveway, indicating a struggle. Though they hadn't been turned on, he could see that they'd decorated their bushes and palm tree with lights. There also weren't any lights on in the house.

There wasn't much Travis hated more than a piece of shit who liked to hurt women. Jumping the last fence, he crept to the side of the one-story home until he reached the metal fence surrounding the backyard. Instead of vaulting over it, he quietly opened the gate. Leaving the door open, he moved silently to the corner of the home, and rounded it into the backyard. He was directly under a window. The curtains were slightly cracked so he grasped the sill and started to push up.

That was when he heard the male voice, slurred and shouting. "Tell me where she is, you stupid whore!" It was followed by a muted crack, like a palm hitting a cheek.

Gritting his teeth, Travis half-stood and peered through the window. A dim light above the stove was the only illumination but it was enough for him to see what was going on. A woman with straight, dark hair and pale skin sat at a round wooden table, clutching her upper arm with her free hand. Her hand was covered in blood and a tall, muscular man wearing a flannel shirt and khakis was waving a gun around and shouting, wanting to know where Juanita was. The woman was crying and shaking her head, mumbling in Spanish.

Shit.

ACKNOWLEDGMENTS

As usual, I owe a big thanks to Kari Walker for reading the early version of this story. Thank you for all your thoughts. I'm grateful to have you in my life—and I'm so happy you love Christmas as much as me. I also owe gratitude to Joan Turner for her attention to detail. As always, thanks to Jaycee of Sweet 'N Spicy Designs for her wonderful design work. To my assistant, Sarah, thank you for everything you do! For my readers, thank you for reading my books. To my parents, who gave me a love of the holiday season early on, thank you. And of course, thank you to my husband and son. I'm eternally grateful for your patience and understanding when I'm locked away in my writing cave. As always, I'm thankful to God for so many opportunities.

COMPLETE BOOKLIST

Red Stone Security Series
No One to Trust
Danger Next Door
Fatal Deception
Miami, Mistletoe & Murder
His to Protect
Breaking Her Rules
Protecting His Witness
Sinful Seduction
Under His Protection
Deadly Fallout
Sworn to Protect
Secret Obsession
Love Thy Enemy
Dangerous Protector

The Serafina: Sin City Series
First Surrender
Sensual Surrender
Sweetest Surrender
Dangerous Surrender

Deadly Ops Series
Targeted
Bound to Danger
Chasing Danger (novella)
Shattered Duty
Edge of Danger
A Covert Affair

121

ABOUT THE AUTHOR

Katie Reus is the *New York Times* and *USA Today* bestselling author of the Red Stone Security series, the Moon Shifter series and the Deadly Ops series. She fell in love with romance at a young age thanks to books she pilfered from her mom's stash. Years later she loves reading romance almost as much as she loves writing it.

However, she didn't always know she wanted to be a writer. After changing majors many times, she finally graduated summa cum laude with a degree in psychology. Not long after that she discovered a new love. Writing. She now spends her days writing dark paranormal romance and sexy romantic suspense.

For more information on Katie please visit her website: www.katiereus.com. Also find her on twitter @katiereus or visit her on facebook at: www.facebook.com/katiereusauthor.

CPSIA information can be obtained
at www.ICGtesting.com
Printed in the USA
BVOW08s1926211216

471542BV00002B/148/P